Christy's Choice

MAUD JOHNSON

SCHOLASTIC INC.
New York Toronto London Auckland Sydney Tokyo

Cover Photo by Owen Brown

ISBN: 0-590-32387-3

12 11 10 9 8 7 6 5 4   3 4 5 6 7/8

Printed in the U.S.A.   06

Christy's Choice

A Wildfire Book

WILDFIRE TITLES
FROM SCHOLASTIC

Love Comes to Anne by Lucille S. Warner
I'm Christy by Maud Johnson
That's My Girl by Jill Ross Klevin
Beautiful Girl by Elisabeth Ogilvie
Superflirt by Helen Cavanagh
A Funny Girl Like Me by Jan O'Donnell
Just Sixteen by Terry Morris
Suzy Who? by Winifred Madison
Dreams Can Come True by Jane Claypool Miner
I've Got a Crush on You by Carol Stanley
An April Love Story by Caroline B. Cooney
Dance with Me by Winifred Madison
One Day You'll Go by Sheila Schwartz
Yours Truly, Love, Janie by Ann Reit
The Summer of the Sky-Blue Bikini by Jill Ross Klevin
I Want to Be Me by Dorothy Bastien
The Best of Friends by Jill Ross Klevin
The Voices of Julie by Joan Oppenheimer
Second Best by Helen Cavanagh
A Kiss for Tomorrow by Maud Johnson
A Place for Me by Helen Cavanagh
Sixteen Can Be Sweet by Maud Johnson
Take Care of My Girl by Carol Stanley
Lisa by Arlene Hale
Secret Love by Barbara Steiner
Nancy & Nick by Caroline B. Cooney
Wildfire Double Romance by Diane McClure Jones
Senior Class by Jane Claypool Miner
Cindy by Deborah Kent
Too Young to Know by Elisabeth Ogilvie
Junior Prom by Patricia Aks
Saturday Night Date by Maud Johnson
He Loves Me Not by Caroline Cooney
Good-bye, Pretty One by Lucille S. Warner
Just a Summer Girl by Helen Cavanagh
The Impossible Love by Arlene Hale
Sing About Us by Winifred Madison
The Searching Heart by Barbara Steiner
Write Every Day by Janet Quin-Harkin
Christy's Choice by Maud Johnson

I

When I opened my eyes, the first thing I saw was a zigzag streak of sunshine on the green wall. *Green?* For a second I was startled. There were no green walls in our house. I tried to move, to turn over in bed, and a weight pulled at my left side. That's when I saw the plaster cast on my left arm.

The fog of sleep cleared out of my brain and yesterday's happenings came rushing back. The bright August morning when my mother and I started out on a shopping trip . . . the automobile accident . . . Mama and I being knocked off the highway by two speeding cars whose drivers were racing . . . the horrible crunch of metal on metal as one of the cars sideswiped us, and then our automobile whirling and whirling through the air half on its side with me doubled up against the door, and Mama, who had been driving, shoved on top of me so that I couldn't move, and the ground coming closer and closer and closer — until there was nothing.

Suddenly, I knew where I was and why the walls were green. I was in a hospital room.

The previous afternoon I'd regained consciousness in the hospital to find my left arm was broken and in a cast, and that I had what the doctors termed a mild concussion, plus a lot of bruises. I remembered, too, the sensation of relief I'd experienced at seeing Dad and Mama beside the bed and learning that my mother was bruised and shaken up, but not seriously injured.

Now, almost twenty-four hours after the accident, it was morning again. Thinking about everything, I shivered involuntarily in the warm room, but at the same moment a good memory replaced the frightening ones. *Mike*. He was the best memory of all. He had come to the hospital as soon as he learned I was hurt.

Mike Maxwell. . . . Like me, he would be a senior at Greenview High School when classes started in September. Lying in the hospital bed that August morning, I closed my eyes and relived his visit of the previous night.

I'd asked Mike how he knew what had happened, since the accident took place on a highway about fifty miles from Greenview, where we lived, and Mama and I were taken to the closest hospital, not the one in our community.

"After your parents left the hospital and were on their way home, they stopped to tell me," he said.

Mike worked at the Greenview Service Station all day in the summer, and on Saturdays and after school during the rest of the year. Dad telephoned the hospital from the service station to ask that Mike be permitted to visit me that evening.

Mike sat by the bed and held my right hand between both of his, worrying aloud because I cried at the sight of him. They weren't wild sobs, just quiet ones with tears gathering in the corners of my eyes. After a while he accepted my explanation that they actually were happy tears since he and I were together. That was the truth. I was more than happy to see him, and having him with me made the pain more bearable.

An hour later I was even happier when he begged the nurse to be allowed to remain past regular visiting hours.

"Couldn't I stay just a little longer?" Mike had pleaded. "Please. Christy and I are — Well, she's my girl and —"

Before he finished the sentence, the nurse shook her head.

Mike kissed me tenderly and whispered, "I'll be back to see you tomorrow, Christy. Thank God you're going to be okay. I couldn't stand it if you weren't."

He had no way of knowing, but until that moment I'd almost given up hope of ever hearing him call me his girl. Oh, sure, we were dating, even going steady now. And I had cared about him for months, drawn to him from the first time I saw him right after my family moved from New York to the small town of Greenview, Virginia, in sight of the Blue Ridge Mountains.

That first afternoon was engraved on my mind. Mama and I had been to the grocery store and we

3

stopped for gas at the Greenview Service Station. Mike, bundled up against the icy cold in a heavy khaki jacket with a black knitted cap which covered his ears, cleaned the windshield with several thicknesses of wet blue paper, his arm moving in a circular motion, around and around, until it almost hypnotized me. When he realized I was watching him through the glass, from the front seat, he grinned and said, "Hi, there."

I rolled the window down and we chatted a little, but I was too shy to say much and I didn't tell him my name or find out his that afternoon. Almost the only fact I learned about him then was that he went to Greenview High where I would be a junior. Afterward, I thought about him a lot although Mike didn't call me immediately. He didn't dislike me. I simply didn't matter to him one way or another, until later.

It was January when my father was transferred to Virginia to manage a plant which manufactured electric motors; back then, Mike was going steady will Jill Rogers. She was a high school junior just as Mike and I were, a breathtakingly beautiful girl with auburn hair flecked with gold and a gorgeous, curving figure. She had only to toss that shining hair and boys gathered around her, but she was Mike Maxwell's girl then and people at school said, "Mike and Jill," or, "Jill and Mike," as if the phrase was one long word instead of three.

Beside Jill, I felt drab and uninteresting, especially since I'd never really dated, and I was terribly ill at ease when I was near a boy. No

4

matter how much I tried, it was impossible not to be envious of Jill when the two of them walked down the school corridors, holding hands, or when I saw her getting into his car. He would drop her off at her house on his way to work.

My feelings about Mike were locked in my heart, a secret I couldn't tell anyone since I never dreamed he'd want to be with me. Yet, the miracle happened. During the spring Mike and I had some casual dates when he and Jill had broken up, and one evening he kissed me in the moonlight in my backyard. Maybe he felt the warm glow I felt because as the end of school neared and final exams loomed before summer vacation, he wasn't dating anybody but me.

In appearance, I was the same Christy Jamison, sixteen years old with brown hair and a figure almost boyishly straight instead of luscious like Jill's. But I had changed. It wasn't something which showed to the world like a new hairdo or an unusual shade of lipstick. The change was *inside* me. I could sense it, feel it subtly. I wasn't as shy as I'd once been, or as nervous when I was around boys. I could chat normally and laugh and be natural in a group rather than becoming tongue-tied.

Knowing Mike made the difference in me. I knew that instinctively just as I knew he cared about me and that I'd see him every single night during the summer as well as sometimes during the days — until September when school reopened and my parents clamped down with their no-dating-on-school-nights rule.

5

Mike had never actually said he loved me or even mentioned our going steady although our friends took it for granted. By midsummer, I was taking it for granted, too, and maybe it was stupid for me not to feel secure about my relationship with him, but I wasn't positive he considered me "his girl" the way he'd once thought of Jill Rogers — until he said it to the nurse when he came to the hospital to see me the night of Mama's and my automobile accident.

II

Dad drove me home from the hospital the afternoon following the accident, bringing Mike with him from Greenview and explaining that my mother wanted to come but he had persuaded her not to make the trip.

"Susan is more sore and stiff today than she'd like to admit," Dad said. "A fifty-mile ride each way might exhaust her when she's still a bit shaky."

"I'm her replacement, Christy," Mike grinned, squeezing my right hand tenderly, his fingers warm against mine.

"Was getting off work a problem?" I asked him.

"I'm not skipping the entire afternoon — only as long as it takes to get you home. Uncle Eb is real understanding about letting his employees off when the reason is valid." Mike's uncle, Eben Maxwell, owned the Greenview Service Station.

Looking at Mike, I longed to have his arms

around me and was sure from the expression in his eyes that he wanted to kiss me, but holding hands was as much affection as we showed in front of other people. I'd have died if he'd kissed me with my father watching or in front of Mama.

The physician who treated me after the accident, Dr. Michaels, issued stern orders when he signed my discharge from the hospital. "A concussion — even a slight one such as you have, Christy — isn't anything to be ignored," he said. "Mother Nature will heal it if you give her the chance, so for the next week you're to do a lot of sitting around and resting. No tennis or swimming or jogging. No dancing, either, for a couple of weeks. If you should feel nauseated or begin to have headaches or feel dizzy, get in touch with a doctor immediately."

I asked about my arm which ached more at the moment than my head did. The plaster cast, which extended from my elbow down to the point where my thumb joined the palm, felt heavy and cumbersome.

"The pain in your arm will wear off gradually," Dr. Michaels replied. "I'm sending the X rays of the break to your doctor in Greenview. He'll keep a check on you and remove the cast in about six weeks if all goes well."

"Six weeks?" I swallowed a sigh. It sounded like a very long time.

The doctor patted my shoulder. "You're right-handed, aren't you? Count your blessings that you broke your left arm and not your right."

"I've counted my blessings about a lot of things in the past twenty-four hours," I murmured.

Dad had brought pillows from home and he insisted on my lying down in the back of the car. He and Mike sat in front, Mike turning sideways, letting one of his arms dangle over the seat. As Dad drove out of the hospital grounds, I touched Mike's hand and realized he'd deliberately put it within my reach. He looked at me, winked, and smiled when my fingers twined with his.

It was a quarter to four when Mike got out of the car at the service station, saying he'd see me later. Dad turned toward our house, which was two miles from town, and I propped myself higher on the pillows to gaze out of the automobile window.

"Know something strange, Dad?" I said. "I feel as if I've been gone a month instead of just two days and a night. Not even two full days. It seems an eternity since Mama and I headed for Roanoke yesterday morning."

"I often have that sensation if I've been out of town on a short business trip and am eager to get home," he answered. "Maybe it's the anticipation of coming home which makes you feel you've been gone longer than you actually have been. People who don't care whether they're home or not probably don't have that reaction."

In the golden sunlight, the Blue Ridge Mountains ringing the road on every side looked intensely blue, living up to their name. The five ranges were outlined against the cloudless August sky with the most distant mountains a pale, smoky color and the nearest one, dark blue. Cows grazed in the rolling valley on either side of the highway, and fields of grain and corn looked lush and green.

A lump came into my throat at the first glimpse of our house. It was a tall, skinny, wooden building painted white with dark green trim, set in a grove of trees on the very top of a hill, and it was old, having been built in the early 1900's, although the kitchen and bathrooms had been modernized. The first time I saw the house back in January, I'd thought it looked odd because of its sharp, vertical lines and its nine bay windows. Crazy windows, Mike called them. But I had come to love the place in the months we'd lived there, especially enjoying those three-sided, "crazy" windows which afforded a view of the mountains from every room including the kitchen.

My mother must have been watching for us, as she came out of the front door before the car was all the way up the hill. I caught my breath because she showed she had been hurt. A purplish-yellow bruise covered most of one of her cheeks, and her mouth was swollen. She and I reached out to hug one another, and for a second I was afraid I was going to cry, but I blinked the tears back.

The remainder of that day formed a pattern for me for the week which followed. As Dr. Michaels ordered, I did a lot of sitting around and resting, and Dad insisted that Mama do the same. She moaned that her garden needed attention, that her flowers and vegetables would become overgrown with weeds, but Dad assured her he would see to the garden, and he did.

My big adjustment was learning to manage without my left arm. I wrapped the cast with plastic when I took a shower, but Mama had to help me shampoo my hair, and when I wore sneakers, she, or whoever was nearby, had to tie the laces. Dad cut my meat into bite-sized mouthfuls at dinner just as he'd done when I was very small, and going to bed meant making sure the arm in the cast was in a comfortable position or I couldn't sleep.

Mike phoned me each morning when there was a lull at the service station, and he was at our house every evening. We watched television and played Scrabble and talked—there was never enough time for us to say everything we wanted to say to each other.

Betsy Collins came to see me a couple of afternoons, and one night she and Gordon Sager paid a visit while Mike was there. They were Mike's and my closest friends, and like us they would be seniors when school opened.

But the best moments came shortly before Mike went home. He and I would walk across the backyard and down the slope toward Mama's garden to the big outcropping of rocks which formed a stone bench. All summer we'd sat on that bench to talk and kiss. Each evening we were holding hands as we left the house, but by the time we'd covered the hundred or more feet to the rocks, one of Mike's arms was around my waist and I was so close to him our sides touched.

During that particular week when I was trying to learn to live with the cast on my arm, the moon was new, a curving, silvery arc which gave off such dim light that the sky was black enough for millions of stars to be visible. Leaves on the tree branches whispered softly overhead and the air was fragrant with the scent of summer flowers. I sensed the beauty of the nights subconsciously without really being aware of anything except the enchanting feel of Mike's mouth on mine.

III

Doing something special with Betsy and Gordon on the last night before school opened was my idea, and when I suggested it to Mike, he answered, "Sure. Sounds great, Christy. You can't go swimming, though. Not with that cast on your arm."

Mike and I were sitting on the glider on my front porch, enjoying the hazy twilight on a Friday evening. School would begin the following Tuesday, the day after the Labor Day holiday.

"You three can swim," I told him. "I'll watch you and Betsy and Gordon. Maybe I'll go wading."

"I hope you're not thinking about heading for Coburn's Lake, Christy." All of a sudden his voice was hard as he mentioned the nearby lake which had picnic facilities as well as a swimming area. "Because if you are," he went on, "I can tell you right now it'll be jammed just like it was the Fourth of July. Everybody in ten counties will

13

have the same idea about winding up summer with a bang."

I turned my face ever so slightly away from him. Coburn's had been in the back of my mind.

"How about a cookout? Or a picnic?" I suggested quickly, mentally ruling Coburn's Lake out. "We could have it here in my yard."

He nodded, smiling, and I relaxed. Going to the lake no longer seemed like a good plan because his mention of the Fourth of July made me cringe. On that holiday, Mike and I teamed up with Bud Warren and his date for the trip to Coburn's which was about twenty miles from Greenview. Betsy had been in Maryland visiting her grandmother at the time, and Gordon had gone there to spend the Fourth with her.

Bud was a long-time friend of Mike's — they'd lived on the same street all of their lives. It was fortunate that Bud was a likable boy with a good sense of humor as he was painfully homely. His head was too small for his sturdy body and his mouth was so wide it made him resemble a cartoon drawing. His ears stuck out and his pale eyes were dwarfed by bushy, straw-colored eyebrows which seemed out of place with his dark brown hair.

Everything about that Fourth of July outing was a disaster. Everything. Mike and I had expected Bud to bring Sharon Park, the girl he'd been dating, but he showed up with Jill Rogers. I felt as if I would explode at having to spend hours with Mike's former girl friend.

14

Mike clammed up, scarcely speaking while we were at the lake except to growl in answer to a direct question. Every now and then I saw him stealing a glance at Jill, and no wonder. With her curving body and long, shapely legs, she was gorgeous in a white bikini which accentuated her tan and her glowing hair.

The lake and the grounds were packed with people of all ages celebrating the Fourth. We couldn't move a foot in any direction without bumping into somebody or having to step over a sunbather or a child, and the concession stand, where we intended buying supper, sold out of everything before we had so much as one crumb to eat. The worst moment of the evening came when we started to Bud's car to go home and a fellow named Carl Browning, a boy Jill apparently knew well, rode by us on a motorcycle and offered her a ride to the parking lot. Laughing outrageously, she hopped up behind him, put on his extra helmet, and they vroomed off.

Even though minutes later she was waiting when Mike, Bud, and I reached the car, it was awful of her to ignore her date and go joyriding with another boy. Mike was as disgusted as I was, and Bud was hurt in addition to being angry. The following night Mike told me he believed Bud finally had gotten Jill Rogers out of his system. It was generally known that Bud had been crazy about her ever since grade school days, but she only dated him if she had nothing more interesting to do or if she wanted him to do something for her.

I hadn't seen Jill since the Fourth. The middle of July my mother and I left Virginia to visit relatives in Indiana, and since then, I certainly hadn't bothered to look up Jill. But sitting beside Mike on the porch glider and glancing obliquely toward him, I was furious with myself for feeling tense just because his reference to Coburn's Lake made me think about the person formerly known as "Mike's girl."

"Hey — are you taking a nap or something, Christy?" Mike's voice jarred me away from the July memories. "You're mighty quiet. I don't think you've said a word for at least five minutes."

My answer was a little lie because I didn't want to talk about Jill. "I was thinking about our preschool plans," I said.

"Preschool plans? That sounds as if our mothers are going to buy us new crayons for kindergarten."

"Hardly. Mike, do you realize we'll be seniors?"

"I'm not sure I'll actually grasp it until I'm in school."

"That's the way I feel, too." I leaned my head against his shoulder and his arm went around me, his cheek resting on my hair. Darkness had fallen and we watched the moon and the stars, contented to be together. It was half an hour before the cookout was mentioned.

"If we have the cookout in your yard, Christy, you tell the rest of us what to bring," Mike said.

16

"I know Betsy will volunteer to make potato salad. She always does and it's always good. I think she must get turned on chopping potatoes and celery."

"Then let her do it. Thank goodness I won't have to chop potatoes and celery."

"I'll provide hamburgers and buns and stuff like mustard and ketchup to go on them," I said. "You guys have spent plenty of money on Betsy and me this summer, so you'll get off easy. One of you can provide Cokes and the other can get something for dessert. Doughnuts or popsicles or whatever."

Mike flashed a saucy grin. "I'm beginning to like these arrangements of yours more and more. Any girl who wants to save my money can't be all bad. Who knows? Maybe you'll amount to something yet, Miss Christina Jamison."

I rumpled his hair and we laughed together.

Mike was serious quickly. "What about Bud?" he asked. "Let's include him. I don't think he's had much fun lately, and from what he says about his summer job, working in the ice cream factory is one huge bore."

"Gordon works there, too, Mike. And he doesn't talk about being bored."

I promptly wished I'd left that remark unsaid. It was true, but Mike's jaw muscles tightened. He was protective about Bud and months earlier I'd decided it must be because Bud was so pitifully homely.

"Gordon has Betsy." Mike's tone was quiet. "It

17

makes a whale of a lot of difference to have someone special. And Bud doesn't."

"You get in touch with Bud and invite him to the cookout." I drew a long breath because there was something I wanted to add and didn't know which words to use to keep from seeming harsh. "If — if Bud brings a girl, I hope he'll choose one who gets along with the rest of us."

Jill's name wasn't mentioned, but Mike knew the person I meant, and to my consternation he defended Jill after a fashion.

"Jill's okay, Christy," he said and shrugged. "Sometimes she does stupid stuff without realizing that she's creating problems. I don't think Bud will ever date her again, though. When she got on Carl Browning's motorcycle the Fourth of July, I guess she ended things with Bud once and for all."

I hope so, I thought silently. *I truly hope so.*

It wasn't that I didn't trust Mike around Jill Rogers, because I did, although I wasn't sure I trusted her. She'd probably like to be dating Mike once more, especially since she wasn't going steady at the moment and hadn't since Vince Halloran had gone to Ohio. She and Vince had a big romance in progress before I moved to Virginia, but he quit high school before he graduated, went to Ohio where his sister lived, and returned to Greenview the previous spring. He and Jill had gone steady again until he left town.

I couldn't forget that Jill had been Mike's girl a lot longer than I had, and she was so beautiful I'd find myself shrinking when I was near her until I seemed to be nothing but bones and skin and misery.

Friends invited Mama and Dad for dinner on Monday, the final night of summer vacation, but my mother helped me get ready for the cookout, which was fortunate as the cast on my arm made me awkward. She and I set up a sawhorse table in the backyard, covering it with a green cloth, and for the centerpiece I filled a brown pottery jug with yellow marigolds and the last of the blue asters from the garden.

We wrapped the hamburger patties in foil and put them in the refrigerator, ready to be cooked. I carried paper cups and plates to the table, and the charcoal was lit in the grill when Betsy and Gordon arrived late in the afternoon. Gordon had brought popsicles as well as doughnuts, and Betsy was carrying a wooden bowl of potato salad which she'd decorated with slivers of red pimento and slices of hard-boiled egg.

"Isn't Mike here yet?" Gordon asked, looking at his watch.

"He phoned around five to say he'd be late," I explained. "He had to take the wrecker out on the highway to tow in a stalled car, and then had to go home and get cleaned up. But he said unless there were problems attaching the car to the wrecker, he didn't think he'd be later than six-fifteen and — Look, there's a car now."

The three of us turned to face the lane which

wound up our hill from the road. I'd caught sight of a dark car — Mike had a twelve-year-old black sedan — but the automobile was lost temporarily from our range of vision when it moved in front of the house before circling to the backyard. As it came into view again, I gasped. It wasn't Mike. Bud Warren was driving, and Jill sat beside him, the late afternoon sun making her hair into a burnished red-gold crown.

"Hi, people," Bud called, braking the car near us without cutting off the motor. "Sorry we can't stay, but Jill promised to baby-sit her brother's kids tonight and she's already late since she was supposed to show up at quarter to six. I told her I'd hang around with her so she won't get lonesome. I tried to phone Mike to tell him, but some guy at the service station said he'd left for the day, so I figured it would be easier to stop by here."

When I opened my mouth, I couldn't utter a sound. It was Gordon who answered Bud.

"Okay," Gordon told him. "We'll see you two at school tomorrow."

Another car turned off the road into our lane, and that time it was Mike. Bud and Jill waved to him as they left, but they didn't stop to speak. Mike, looking freshly scrubbed in clean jeans and a yellow knitted shirt and with shower water clinging to his hair, glued his eyes to my face as he got out of his car and strolled to where I stood. I hadn't moved since seeing Bud and Jill.

"What was that all about?" Mike asked gruffly.

Gordon glanced at me and when I remained silent, he answered Mike. I knew I must look as stunned as I felt.

"When I invited Bud to come here tonight, he told me he didn't have a date lined up." Mike, continuing to stare at me, sounded almost apologetic. "I — uh — guess his plans got changed."

I came to my senses. I didn't know if the expression in Mike's eyes caused it or if the shock of seeing Bud with Jill was wearing off. I realized that the cookout was in *my* yard and that nobody would have a good time unless *I* put the latest Jill Rogers episode where it belonged — in the file of unimportant matters. If Bud was dumb enough to allow himself to be hurt all over again by Jill, that was his problem.

Smiling wasn't difficult as I said, "The charcoal is ready. Let's begin cooking."

There was one brief reference to Jill and Bud later in the evening after we'd eaten and the sawhorse table was cleared and dismantled. We were sitting on the grass, Gordon and Betsy holding hands, while my back rested against an oak tree and Mike lay full length on the ground with his head in my lap. I smoothed his hair away from his forehead and once when I stopped, he said, "Keep it up, Christy. Keep it up forever. I like that."

The day had been warm but darkness brought a cool breeze across the mountains and I could almost smell the approach of autumn. Apples were ripening in a nearby orchard and the tangy scent of chrysanthemums drifted up to us from Mama's garden. The moon hadn't risen and the only light in the yard came from a lamp in the living room, its pale lemony glow shining through one of the bay windows to accent the night around us.

When an owl hooted, Gordon imitated the sound and all of us laughed.

"Watch it, fella," Mike said. "You might be giving that bird a mating call."

"That's his problem, not mine," Gordon quipped.

Our laughter rang out again before we settled into a comfortable silence. I moved my fingers from Mike's forehead down his cheek to his chin, tracing the outline of his jaw. Reaching up, he caught my hand and kissed the palm.

Betsy's voice broke the magic spell. "I thought I'd pass out this afternoon after I saw Jill with Bud," she said. "When did they start dating again?"

"Tonight, I guess," Gordon answered. "After all, Bud told Mike he didn't have a date for tonight, and now he's with Jill — and driving her to a baby-sitting job and hanging around, no less. That was her idea, I know. After she gets those kids of her brother's to sleep, she's probably bored stiff trying to entertain herself."

"It would depress anybody to spend the last night of summer vacation alone and that goes double for Jill. She doesn't enjoy being without a guy," Betsy observed.

"You could be right." Mike's voice was low

and I didn't know if his statement was for Gordon or Betsy.

I didn't say anything.

A car turned from the road into our lane, its headlights making two bright slashes through the black night as it came up the hill.

"Christy, I think your folks are home," Gordon remarked as if the rest of us weren't aware of it.

"Yes, they are," I murmured, relieved at any interruption which ended the talk of Jill.

IV

Mike was waiting when I stepped off the school bus the following morning. He leaned against the corner of the building, a smile curving his mouth as soon as he spotted me, and we said, "Hi," to each other at the same moment. His eyes went immediately to the tan canvas tote bag in my right hand. My left arm, still in the cast, rested in a sling tied at the back of my neck.

"I would have carried your books and stuff for you if you'd given me the chance," he said, and he seemed almost hurt that I was managing without his help.

Monday night after Betsy and Gordon went home from the cookout, Mike and I joined Mama and Dad in the den to watch the news on TV, and when the program ended, Mike stood up to go and said, "I'll pick you up for school in the morning, Christy."

Dad spoke at once, before I had a chance to do it. "I think it will be best if you use the school bus in the mornings, Christy."

24

"But —" I was about to tell him I'd much rather ride with Mike.

"You can't go in Mike's car one day and on the bus the next because the bus schedules have to include regular stops," Dad continued. "Later on, when winter weather sets in, and there'll be a lot of it in these mountains, Mike may have enough of a problem getting himself to school on time in the mornings without coming this far out of his way."

"If we have snow or ice, I can always use the jeep from the service station," Mike cut in.

Dad remained firm. My mother said nothing although I had the feeling she and Dad must have discussed this in advance. Neither of them had mentioned it to me, though.

I could guess what was going through their minds and it wasn't that they disliked Mike or didn't trust him, but my parents had a thing about punctuality, and they knew I'd reach school on time if I rode the bus. I'd much rather have gone with Mike, but I was aware of the mornings when he overslept and barely made school by the final bell.

After the conversation about the school bus, Mike said good night to my parents and we went outside for a last kiss. Darkness swirled about us as we paused on the back steps. I didn't realize how tense he was until I touched his shoulder. His muscles were rigid.

"Mr. Jamison has a point," he muttered fiercely. "But I'd still like to pick you up tomorrow, Christy."

"I know . . ." I stood on tiptoe to kiss him. "But you can bring me home tomorrow before you go to work like you did the last month of the spring term, can't you? And do it all the other afternoons? I'll tell the bus driver that I'll be on the list to ride in the mornings but not in the afternoons."

"You bet I will," he said and returned my kiss.

Walking into the school building with Mike Tuesday morning, I noticed the way his jaw tightened after his comment about carrying my books. While I was wondering about it, he spilled everything out.

"I guess I like to believe you need me every now and then," he said in a thick voice.

"Mike, I do! You should know that! Not to carry my books, though." Fitting my right hand into his, I let the tote bag dangle from my wrist and swing between us. "There's not a chance you and I will have identical class schedules. When I have a load of books using the bag will make it easier for me until the cast comes off my arm."

His face softened. "You've convinced me, Christy," he whispered and flashed the smile I'd come to adore.

A feeling of tenderness for him swept over me. Mike had been unusually protective since the automobile accident, and it was wonderful to have him show his concern and caring, but I didn't know how to handle his possessiveness. Trying to understand a boy's thinking was new to me since I didn't have any brothers and had never really dated before Mike came into my life.

At Greenview High freshmen were assigned to a homeroom and kept it the entire time they were enrolled, with the teachers laughingly saying they, too, were "promoted" every year as students progressed up the ladder toward becoming seniors. When Mike and I reached the stairs at school that Tuesday, we went in opposite directions as we weren't in the same homeroom. Mine, No. 218, had been given a fresh coat of paint and new window shades during the summer, and Mrs. Perkins, the teacher, stood by the door to greet each student by name.

All high schools probably have the same sort of commotion on opening day with noise, laughter, chatter, the hubbub of everyone trying to locate newly assigned lockers and the inevitable schedule mix-ups. I had only been at Greenview High since January, but somehow, on that September Tuesday when the fall term began, it really was *my* school. I belonged there, and was happy to belong, a contrast to the loneliness and apprehension I'd experienced my first month in Virginia. Smiling to myself as I settled into my familiar seat in Mrs. Perkins's room, it was hard to realize this was the beginning of my final year of high school.

We had ten-minute class periods that first day and were dismissed at noon. Mike and I compared schedule cards when we passed in the hall, seeing that we only had two classes together but were lucky enough to be assigned the same lunch period. We arranged to meet at the rear entrance when the final bell rang, and I reached the spot first, knowing there would be a brief wait as my last class was just across the hall while his was at the far end of the building.

Several students I knew casually walked by and we exchanged greetings. I heard Jill's tinkling laughter before I saw her and I turned my head in the direction of the sound because I couldn't stop myself. She was coming down the corridor with Carl Browning, and she was as beautiful as ever. A lanky boy with lots of dark curly hair, Carl was the one who had given her the motorcycle ride on the Fourth of July.

I spoke first. I made myself do it since the previous night when she and Bud drove into my backyard, I hadn't said a word to her and I didn't want to be rude twice. She and Carl were so wrapped up in each other they might not have noticed me if I hadn't uttered their names, and I hoped my voice seemed more natural to them than it sounded to my ears.

"Hi-ya, Christy," Carl answered.

Without removing her eyes from his face, Jill said, "Oh, hello," flinging the words over her shoulder to me. She was so impersonal I had the feeling she'd probably use that same tone if she was closing the door in the face of a persistent salesman.

They stepped out into the parking lot before Mike rushed up, full of apologies for making me wait. He explained that a cabinet in his last-period class was jammed and he'd stayed to take the door off its hinges for the teacher. That was Mike, I thought to myself, pleased that he was the sort of boy who was always willing to help anybody who needed it.

Bud Warren was with Mike. Taking a long breath, I wondered what Bud's reaction would have been if he'd appeared two minutes earlier and seen Jill with Carl.

"Want to go to Sonny's and grab a sandwich?" Mike asked me. Sonny's was a soda shop in downtown Greenview and a favorite spot for teenagers.

"Love to," I told him, making a mental note to phone home from Sonny's and tell Mama not to count on me for lunch.

"Bud's coming with us," Mike added.

At the moment I would rather have had Mike to myself instead of sharing him with Bud, but I didn't say so. The three of us climbed into Mike's car, sitting in the front seat with me between the two guys. A thought sped through my mind that only a couple of hours before I'd silently questioned Mike's being possessive of me, while now, I was just as possessive as he was, only in a different way.

V

Autumn came slowly to the mountains with a few scattered trees turning yellow or red as the summer heat evaporated to make comfortably pleasant days, and nights which were deliciously cool. One morning the end of September as I was dressing for school, glanced through the bay window in my room, and was astonished to see a blaze of color on the horizon. The mountains were no longer blue, but they had been changed by the leaves into a tapestry of golds and crimsons and rich burgundies.

There were other signs of fall. Apple trees were heavy with fruit. Pumpkins, fat and orange, dotted a field across the road from our hill, and beyond the pumpkin patch, the corn was brown, the stalks standing lopsided while they waited to be cut for silage. Berries on the dogwoods glowed as red as Christmas candles, and in our yard, prickly brown balls from the sweet gum trees littered the grass.

Chrysanthemums were still blooming in Mama's garden, but the other flowers were gone and so were most of the summer vegetables. Cucumber and bean vines had dried up, their leaves curling against the string trellis which supported them, and the few tomatoes which continued to grow looked oddly out of place on the drooping plants. The first killing frost was due sometime between the middle and the end of October, my mother said after consulting her almanac, and it would finish off her garden.

Before that happened, there were two major events in my life. The first was my birthday. *Seventeen!* I could scarcely believe it.

As my birthday neared and Mike didn't say a word about it, I wasn't sure he remembered the day since the only time we'd discussed it was back in March before we knew each other well. That conversation had come in Math when Mr. Hansen, the teacher, was summoned to the office to take a long-distance phone call, and with the teacher gone, students began talking. I was in front of Mike as we were seated in alphabetical order and there were no L's or K's in that particular class and no other J's or M's.

I'd turned sideways in my seat, hoping Mike would speak to me and he did, asking me when I would be seventeen, giving me a quizzical look which made me feel about twelve. He had to realize I was at least sixteen because I had a driver's license.

"October," I answered.

His mouth formed a half-smile. "I've already reached that ripe old age," he said, explaining that he had been seventeen for nine days.

He seemed to expect me to say something and I tried desperately to come up with a cute remark, something interesting enough to make him laugh. I had to settle for, "Happy late birthday, Mike," which wasn't particularly clever.

Mulling over the conversation in my mind that evening when I was curled up on the window seat in my room, I realized it wouldn't have mattered what I said because Mike was going steady with Jill at the time and I was merely a girl who happened to sit in front of him in Math.

My life changed after Mike and I started dating in the late spring, and as summer slipped into September, I didn't mention that my birthday was in October. But on the final night I was sixteen, it dawned on me that my parents hadn't made even one remark about the approaching birthday, and that was a shock. I'd just finished studying and was in my room, about to undress for bed, when the realization struck, and a strange little ache began in the bottom of my stomach.

Surely Mama and Dad hadn't forgotten, I told myself. Didn't parents always remember the month, day, and year — even the hour — their children were born, especially if it was only one child rather than several? Perhaps my mother thought seventeen was too old for a celebration. I certainly didn't expect balloons and crepe paper streamers or a cake with pink icing, the way we marked the event when I was small, although it hurt to think there might not be a single mention of my birthday.

I shouldn't have been concerned. When I came downstairs the next morning, a cardboard sign that read, "Happy 17th Birthday, Christy," the words written in green ink, was propped against my juice glass on the breakfast table, and we were having French toast, one of my favorites. Two boxes wrapped in colorful flowered paper and tied with green ribbon were beside my plate.

"I was afraid you'd forgotten," I murmured after Mama and Dad gave me what they called special birthday hugs.

"How could I forget the prettiest baby in the universe who arrived right in the middle of the World Series?" Dad said with a grin. "I was watching the ball game on a TV set in the fathers' waiting room at the hospital — and it was the crucial game of the Series — when the doctor came in and told me I had a daughter and I could have a look at her. Know something, Christy? It was hours before I bothered to find out who won that baseball game."

I smiled at him and at Mama. I'd heard the story before and loved hearing it again.

One box held a purse I'd admired in a store window some weeks earlier, and in the other box there was a lovely white blouse made out of silky material. I held it up, remarking wistfully that I couldn't try it on because the cast on my arm was too bulky to slide through the long sleeve.

"Just be patient a little longer, Christy," Dad said. "That cast won't be with you forever."

He was right, of course. It just *seemed* like forever.

School that day was routine. Mike was in his usual spot when I stepped off the bus and he came forward to meet me, lifting the tote bag from my right hand. He didn't say anything about the day being special and I tried to pretend it wasn't as we went through the familiar schedule of classes.

I couldn't forget it was my birthday, though, and I must have reminded myself half a dozen times that it was childish to feel even a trifle disappointed. If the birthday meant so much, I told myself, I should have said something about it in advance to Mike, shouldn't I? There was no satisfactory answer to that question.

Mike dropped me off at home after school and headed for the service station. I went in the house to find my mother in the kitchen spreading pink icing on a cake.

"You remembered," I said, wishing wistfully that Mike could have a slice.

"Didn't you think I would? You've always had pink icing on your birthday cakes." Mama scooped a pink glob with the spatula and held it out to me for a taste. I slid the icing off the utensil with two fingers.

"Mmmmmm . . . yummy," I told her, licking my fingertips.

"Christy, why don't you do your homework right now? You don't want to have to study tonight since it's your birthday, do you?"

I ought to have caught on that something was

34

going to happen that evening despite the casual way she tossed the suggestion at me, but I didn't. Upstairs in my room, I sat down at the desk, glad I'd completed Math homework in study hall at school. Luckily, my other assignments weren't very complicated.

The October days were noticeably shorter. The sun was out of sight behind the mountains and the sky splashed with pink and apricot a couple of hours later when I finished the homework. Already the sunset was fading. A glance through the bay window in my room showed Dad's car turning from the road into our lane which meant we would eat soon as he was always ravenous when he came home at night.

The cast prevented me from giving Mama a lot of help in the kitchen, but at least I could set the table. I brushed my hair and put on fresh lipstick, and on turning from the mirror, glanced through the window once more. Day was nearly gone, the sunset colors now a pearly lavender. Another car was coming up our hill, its headlights glowing through the dusk, and when the car stopped, I smiled. It was too dark for me to see the driver's face but I recognized the silhouette and the walk.

Mike!

I ran out of my room, but Mama had already gone to the front door to let Mike in, and for a second I couldn't absorb what I was seeing.

Mike lived in jeans and knitted sports shirts unless it was for a big occasion, but that night he had on gray slacks with a white shirt and a red-

and-gray striped necktie. When he brought me home from school three hours earlier, he'd said, "See you tomorrow, Christy," but here he was, coming into my house, and from the expression on my mother's face, I knew she'd been expecting him.

He looked up the stairs to where I stood and said, "Hi, there."

My heart did a flip-flop.

"Is anybody around here celebrating something?" Mike went on in a solemn voice although his eyes were full of merriment.

"I'm not," Mama answered. She looked at me and laughed.

"I'm not, either." Mike couldn't suppress a smile any longer. "Unless Mr. Jamison is, I guess that leaves you, Christy."

I didn't speak for a moment because I couldn't, but I was smiling as broadly as Mike was. Mama vanished into the kitchen and I guess Dad was in the den as TV voices sounded from that part of the house. My eyes were riveted to Mike as I came slowly down the stairs.

"Happy Birthday," he whispered.

On the bottom step, I paused. That made my face on a level with his. "How did you know, Mike?"

"I have my methods."

"You didn't mention it at school."

"If you want all the facts, last July when you came home from Indiana, I asked your mother when your birthday was, and she told me. I circled the date on my calendar. Then, last week Mrs. Jamison stopped at the service station one afternoon and invited me to dinner tonight, but she said not to let you know because she wanted it to be a surprise. So, here I am. Are you surprised?"

"You know I am."

I couldn't stop smiling. He took a small package from the pocket of his trousers and handed it to me. Opening the box, I lifted out a thin gold chain so fragile that when I held it up I felt as if I was touching a golden cobweb.

"Mike, it's beautiful," I said. "Help me put it on."

He undid the clasp and slipped the chain around my neck. A mirror hung over the hall table and I looked at my reflection, seeing the gold glimmering against my skin.

"If you'd rather have something else," he said, "it can be exchanged."

"Oh, no! I don't want anything else. I love it."

Tenderness shone in his face. "Save a little of that love for me, Christy. Okay?"

It wasn't necessary to reply with words. He knew I would.

The remainder of my birthday was a happy blur. Mama had gone to a lot of trouble with dinner, cooking dishes she knew I especially liked, using the good china, putting candles on the table. Mike was enough at home with my family to feel at ease and from time to time I let my gaze move around the table to him and to my parents, cherishing all of them and marveling that I'd been gloomy during the morning.

The second major event for me during the first week of October came on the Saturday after my birthday. The doctor removed my cast.

"Take care of that arm, young lady," he cautioned me. "For the next ten days don't lift anything heavier than two or three pounds with your left hand and don't knock your arm against furniture or the wall. Your X rays show the bones have knit well, but it doesn't hurt to be careful. You wouldn't want to break it again."

"I certainly wouldn't," I said, stunned at how strange it seemed to be without the cast. I hadn't realized the weight of it changed the way my body balanced.

Mike and I went to the movies that night. A lot of times on weekends we did something with other people, but on that Saturday it was just the two of us, which suited me. After the movie we stopped at Sonny's for hamburgers, and while the place was filled, we didn't find any of our close friends. Gordon had missed Thursday and Friday from school because he had a virus, and Betsy had gone with Mike and me to the high school football game Friday night. I figured she was at Gordon's house Saturday if he'd stopped being contagious, and heaven only knew where Bud Warren was.

Sonny's had no table service and when Mike went to the food counter for our hamburgers, I glanced around, seeing Carl Browning sitting with five boys. I recognized three of them from school although I didn't know the others.

I would have expected Carl to be dating on a Saturday night, and to see him without a girl made me wonder about Jill and what she was doing. If she wasn't with Carl, had they broken up? Could she possibly be dating Bud? No matter how much she had hurt Bud in the past, I had an idea he'd jump for joy if she contacted him.

Mike returned to our table and I started to ask him about it, but changed my mind. There was no point in spoiling our good time by discussing Jill.

After we left Sonny's, neither of us talked much on the ride to my house. The car radio played softly and I sat close to him, his arm around me and my hand resting on his knee. Without the cast, I could wear my new blouse, and the gold chain was around my neck.

Night made the air cooler and when we got out of the car in my yard, I shivered involuntarily. The cardigan I was wearing was knitted of light-weight yarn.

"Cold?" Mike asked.

"Not really. It's too lovely a night to go inside yet. Did you ever see so many stars?"

"Nope. Never did. If you're cold, I'll keep you warm." He slipped his arms around me and I leaned against him, conscious of the firm, steady way his heart was beating.

"Thank goodness you have two arms now," he whispered.

"I've always had two arms."

"Well, lately one arm and one broken wing."

"Mike, I didn't realize it annoyed you."

"Annoyed me?" He pulled back, loosening his arms a little. "You've got to be kidding, Christy! The real reason I'm glad it's gone is sort of selfish."

"Selfish? You aren't making sense."

"Now you can put two arms around me instead of one arm and a hunk of plaster." His teeth were very white in the darkness when he smiled. "You might need a lesson in hugging after all this time with the cast, though. Want to give it a try and see if you've forgotten how to do it?"

I clasped my hands at the back of his neck, melting closer to him and then forcing myself to pull away.

"Did I pass the test, teacher?" I asked, pretending to be serious.

"Yep. Your grade is A-plus. However, another lesson wouldn't do any harm. Haven't you ever heard of continuing education?"

That made both of us laugh out loud before he kissed me. *I never knew I could be this happy*, I thought.

VI

At noon on the first Monday in November, Mrs. Perkins came to the cafeteria to ask if she could speak to me outside. Mike and I were still at a table although we'd finished lunch and were gabbing with other students, all of us waiting for the bell.

I jumped up and gave Mike a puzzled glance as I followed my homeroom teacher down the corridor to an empty classroom. Frightening thoughts crowded into my brain. If something awful had happened to Mama or Dad, and Mrs. Perkins was the one who had to tell me —

"Don't look so panicky, Christy," she said with a smile, reading my mind as she sat down and motioned me to a seat next to her. "This isn't bad news."

I said, "Oh," and relaxed slightly.

"If I'd asked you to wait after school, I was afraid I'd cause you to miss your ride," she went on. "And there's no possibility of a private conversation during homeroom period in the mornings. I want to know if you're interested in a job for weekends from now until Christmas."

"I certainly am!" I said.

"Are you familiar with Carlyle's Gift Shop on Main Street?"

I nodded. It was a small store with attractive merchandise. I had been there a number of times with my mother.

"Sam Carlyle, who owns that shop, is a neighbor of mine," she explained. "He's enlarging his business, adding a book department to sell a few hardcovers, but mostly paperbacks, and he wants a high school student to work Thursday and Friday afternoons and all day Saturdays, as well as the full week before Christmas after school is closed for the holidays. He hopes having a teenager working there will entice other students into the shop."

"Do you mean I'll have a chance for that job, Mrs. Perkins?"

"Sam asked me to recommend a girl who is conscientious and is enough of a reader to have opened a book when it wasn't just for a school assignment. Are you interested?"

"Oh, yes! Yes!"

"Fine, Christy. I think you'll be exactly what he wants. Sam can't talk with you today, but he'd like to interview you tomorrow. Can you go by the store to see him after school tomorrow?"

As I gave her another eager, "Yes," the class bell rang. Both of us got to our feet.

"One more thing," she added. "Don't let word about this job get out of school. If you and Sam don't come to terms, I'll recommend someone else, but he doesn't want to be deluged with applications."

"I'll have to tell my parents, Mrs. Perkins."

"Of course. You should talk it over with them." She smiled once more. "And I rather think you'll probably want to tell Mike Maxwell, but don't mention it to anybody else until after your interview with Sam."

My face was suddenly steaming. Students knew Mike and I were going steady, but I hadn't realized teachers also knew. My cheeks continued to burn halfway through the next class.

When school was over, Mike was waiting for me beside his car, as usual, and he was full of questions. I hadn't seen him since lunch.

"What did Mrs. Perkins want?" he asked immediately. "She didn't look mad when she came in the cafeteria to get you so I don't suppose you've done anything sinful, but she sure acted mysterious."

I told him, cautioning him to keep it to himself. His lips pursed into a silent whistle as he started the car engine and drove away from the school parking lot.

"Wow! Having a job drop into your lap is great, Christy," he said.

"It isn't in my lap yet. What if Mr. Carlyle doesn't like me?"

"He will. How could he help liking you?"

I squeezed his arm. "Mike, you're prejudiced. He'll see me differently from the way you do."

43

"He darn well better! Sam Carlyle is old enough to be your father."

Mike sounded positively ferocious, and I laughed. He took his eyes off the traffic to glance my way and grinned, mumbling something about not realizing he'd come on so strong.

"Do you know Mr. Carlyle?" I asked.

"Not well. I know his son, Lee, though. Lee is two or three years older than I am. When you're kids, that's a lot of difference, so we never saw much of each other. He finished Greenview High a couple of years ago and was a big ball player. Lettered in three sports. But he wasn't good enough to rate an athletic scholarship and that made him veto college. He went to Kentucky to work for some relatives, I think, but I heard this fall he was back in town and going to the community college."

Mike turned the car into our lane. In a very few minutes he would be leaving to go to the service station.

"I'm scared," I said softly. "I want this job so much I can taste it. I don't think I could stand it if Mr. Carlyle turned me down."

As he braked by our back steps, Mike put his arm around me. "Don't think negative thoughts, Christy. If Mrs. Perkins hadn't believed you could handle the job, I'm positive she'd never have given your name to Mr. Carlyle. I'll phone you tonight and give you a pep talk to keep your morale up."

For a second I pressed my forehead against his

cheek. "It's nice having you for a cheering section, Mike."

"Anytime."

We looked deeply into each other's eyes before we kissed, and I had to make myself leave the car. I didn't want him to go, but neither did I want to make him late for work.

Mama and Dad were thrilled at the news of my job offer although, oddly enough, instead of their reaction making me more self-confident, it had the opposite effect. If I couldn't sell myself during the interview and wasn't hired, I'd not only upset myself, but disappoint all the people who cared about me. My parents . . . Mike . . . even Mrs. Perkins.

The next morning I took a lot of pains dressing, since I was going straight from school to the gift shop. I put on a tan corduroy skirt, which was new, and a tailored white blouse with tiny tan dots. At breakfast Mama offered to come to school for me, saying she would wait in the car while I was being interviewed.

I shook my head. "Thanks, Mama, but Mike said he'd drop me off at the gift shop," I told her, not wanting to say aloud that I needed those few minutes with him to renew my courage. "I'll want a ride home after it's over, though."

"Call me as soon as you're ready," she said. "I'll be here at the house. And, good luck, Christy."

Mike also wished me good luck when he

stopped his car at Carlyle's Gift Shop that afternoon. With a final tug at his fingers, I forced a smile and told myself to be very, very calm as I walked away from him, although my heart was beating twice as fast as usual.

I had been inside the shop enough times to know how it looked, with shelves against the walls to display china and crystal, while bric-a-brac, brass, and wooden items were on tables. That afternoon the first thing I noticed was the empty space in the rear of the shop, a section with bare shelves.

A saleslady who appeared to be about my mother's age came forward and said, "May I help you?" I remembered that she'd waited on Mama and me some weeks earlier when we were selecting a wedding gift. She was plumpish with dark hair and a warm smile.

"My name is Christy Jamison," I replied, thankful that for once my voice wasn't squeaking the way it sometimes did if I was nervous. "I'd like to see Mr. Carlyle."

"He's expecting you. Go straight back through the door at the rear of this room and he'll either be in his office on the right or in the stockroom on the left."

Following her directions, I found myself in the stockroom where a balding, heavyset man was taking armloads of paperback books out of a cardboard crate. He saw me at once and spoke before I could.

"You must be Christy," he said, and something about his tone made me like him instantly.

"Yes, I am. Mr. Carlyle?"

"Right. Did Grace Perkins tell you about the job?"

"She told me a little," I answered. "Enough to make me hope I can work for you."

He smiled, leading me into a cubbyhole office just large enough for a desk, filing cabinets, and two chairs. I'm not sure what I expected during the interview, a lot of questions and maybe even a written test similar to exams at school, I guess, but it wasn't like that at all. Mr. Carlyle and I chatted casually about Greenview and the high school football team, everything so impersonal I didn't realize until I was at home later in the afternoon that he must have used the conversation to size me up.

"Christy, I've shifted merchandise around to make space, and the book department will be in the back, behind the gift section. That's the area which is vacant now," he said and he also mentioned the pay. "I hope we can begin selling books this weekend, and with Christmas coming in just two months, I'm anticipating enough book business to keep you busy. Mrs. Gibson, the lady you passed at the front of the shop, will show you the ropes and tell you about the cash register and how to write up charge slips. Later on, my son, Lee, will be working here afternoons and Saturdays."

He gestured through the open door to the stockroom and I saw books stacked on a long table. "A good bit of the book merchandise has arrived," he went on. "Do you think you could start work day after tomorrow? That's Thursday."

47

"You mean I'm hired?" I gasped.

His smile changed to a chuckle. "I certainly hope so, Christy."

So much excitement rippled through me it was all I could do to sit still. "Yes, I can start Thursday," I said.

"I'll expect you here by three-thirty Thursday which should give you enough time to leave school without breaking your neck hurrying. We close at six every day, and on Saturdays, the store opens at nine o'clock. Wear comfortable shoes, Christy. You'll be on your feet most of the time."

I don't think I walked out of Carlyle's Gift Shop that afternoon. I must have floated or danced or skipped, and I longed to stand on the street corner and shout to the world just because I felt so good. It was only three blocks to the Greenview Service Station and I went there to telephone my mother, although I could have called from any number of places nearer the gift shop.

As I neared the service station, I saw Mike immediately. He was at the gas pumps filling a customer's tank, and I waved to him but didn't pause since he was busy. His Uncle Eb said hello and the two mechanics nodded as I headed for the phone booth on the outside of the building. All of them knew I was Mike's girl, although I seldom stopped at the station unless I was driving Mama's car and needed gas or oil. My father had given me strict orders about staying away from Mike when he was working.

But that particular afternoon was special. I didn't plan to linger at the service station or take Mike away from his work, but I simply had to give him my news.

As I dropped coins into the phone slot and dialed our number, somebody came up behind me and Mike's familiar hand touched my shoulder.

"Christy, you must have landed the job," he said. "I've never seen anyone smile like you're doing."

VII

Mike told me on Thursday morning, my first working day, that his uncle had decided to close the service station at five-thirty in the afternoons during winter.

"Uncle Eb and I probably won't get away before quarter to six or a little later," he said, "but that will be just right for me to pick you up and take you home on the days you work, since you'll get off at six. I'll park as near the gift shop as I can, and you be on the lookout for me."

When I left the shop that first day, twilight had gone and the street lights and automobile headlights sliced into the early November darkness. I was so full of my job I fairly bubbled as I got into the car with Mike.

"It seems almost sinful to get paid for doing something as much fun as working for Mr. Carlyle," I said. "There's a new thrill every time I ring up a sale on the cash register."

"You like it, huh?" He grinned.

"Oh, do I ever! You wouldn't believe how

many paperbacks I sold today. It was fantastic! I was busy almost the whole time."

"I'll believe anything you tell me," he came back. "We're still taking in the school football game tomorrow night, aren't we?"

"I'm counting on it, Mike."

We hadn't missed a single home game for our high school team during the autumn and the season was almost over with just two games left on the schedule. The kickoff was always at eight o'clock Fridays which would give me ample time to go home after work and eat dinner.

Mama and Dad asked more detailed questions that first night than Mike had done, and at school the following day, Betsy was frankly envious. I had an idea other girls might feel as she did, which was a new experience for me. I'd never before had anything other girls wanted. At least, not that I knew about.

Except Mike, I added silently to myself. Remembering how I felt when Mike was dating Jill, when the longing to be with him was a permanent ache inside of me, I wondered if, now that Mike and I were going steady and I also had a job, some of the girls at school wished they were in my place. I didn't feel smug about it, though, and I was determined not to let my incredible luck make me cocky or brittle the way beauty and the ability to attract boys affected Jill Rogers's relationship with girls.

At school Friday during homeroom period I made a point of telling Mrs. Perkins how much I liked the job, thanking her for recommending me.

51

"Sam is impressed with you, Christy," she said. "He couldn't believe a high school girl would have the poise you have, but I reminded him you've lived in a number of different places and that's bound to be a factor."

So, some good had come of my moving a lot, after all. Recalling how I loathed the way the company my father was with transferred us, I was suddenly glad for those moves. Perhaps I'd been able to hide my shyness from Mr. Carlyle, I thought, and then it dawned on me I was chiefly shy around boys, that I could chat with girls my own age and with adults. At first it had been terribly hard for me to carry on a conversation with Mike in spite of wanting very much to do it.

I left the gift shop a few minutes after six on my first Saturday of working. Mike was parked across the street and I was so tired I almost collapsed getting into the car with him.

"Are you okay?" he burst out. "I don't think I've ever heard you sigh, Christy, and you just did."

"I'm pooped and my feet are killing me," I admitted. "I've been standing up the entire day except for a few minutes to eat lunch, and I gobbled that. It's good Mama suggested my bringing a sandwich from home because there wasn't time to go out, not as busy as we were."

"Welcome to the real world." A faint trace of sarcasm sounded in his voice, or maybe I was so tired I imagined it.

"Working is still fun, though," I added.

"What do you want to do tonight, Christy?"

"Take off my shoes. Put on jeans and stay home and watch TV. With you, of course."

"Man-oh-man-oh-man! You haven't had that job any time at all — just two afternoons and one full day — and it's already making an old lady out of you."

"Don't tease me, Mike. I guess it never occurred to me I'd be this exhausted since the work is enjoyable, but now I can see why Dad wants to flop on the couch when he comes home at dinnertime, and why sometimes you're awfully silent at the end of the day if you've been really busy at the service station."

He put his arm around my shoulders and steered the car with his free hand. I leaned against him, some of my fatigue ebbing away at his nearness.

"You'll get used to it soon," he said in a comforting voice. "Next Saturday won't be nearly as rough on you as today was. Before long, you'll be taking these Saturdays in stride."

VIII

A tall, blond man wearing jeans and a blue plaid shirt was coming from the stockroom pushing a shopping cart loaded with paperbacks when I reached the gift shop Saturday morning two weeks later.

"Hi, Christy," he said. "I'm Lee Carlyle. Dad told me to bring these books out so you can put them where they're supposed to be. Okay to dump them on this counter?"

He already knew my name. We exchanged smiles and I murmured, "Put them anywhere," noting that he didn't "dump" the books but carefully stacked them in neat piles. He had an athletic build, his shoulders broad and his waist trim, the rolled-up sleeves of his shirt revealing muscular arms. Lee was as tall as Mike and almost as handsome although in a different way, his tawny hair and light hazel eyes a contrast to Mike's dark coloring. Mike's hair was brown and his eyes were the exact smoky gray-blue of the Blue Ridge Mountains in the sunshine.

"How do you like working here, Christy?" Lee asked.

"Love it." As I spoke, I began placing paper-backs on the shelves to fill the empty spots left from Friday afternoon's sales. "Your father told me you'd be working here soon."

"I am, as of today."

"You're needed if business continues as good as it was Thursday and yesterday."

He finished stacking the books and paused, his hands on the handle of the shopping cart.

"I'd have been here sooner except that this fall I had a temporary job helping the coach at the community college after classes and on Satur-days."

"That sounds interesting," I came back just to be saying something.

"It wasn't the world's biggest deal, but it was all right. The community college is where I'm going to school for the time being, and after the coach hired me last September, I was obligated to hang in through football season. Now, though, Dad —"

Our conversation came to a quick end in the middle of his sentence as the first customer of the day arrived, an elderly lady who wanted help in locating a certain book. As I found the book, slipped it into a paper bag, and rang up the sale on the cash register, I reflected to myself that Lee Carlyle was likable and easy to chat with — or, maybe at last I was reaching the point where talking to a boy didn't paralyze my vocal cords and make my knees shake.

Greenview residents must have plunged into their Christmas shopping early, even though it was just the middle of November, or now that the winter days were short and cold, perhaps they were reading more. The books in Mr. Carlyle's shop were selling. A lot of teenagers bought books from me as well as adults, and the Saturday I met Lee, there wasn't a break during the morning. I didn't talk to Lee again until lunchtime.

Shortly before one o'clock, Mr. Carlyle took over my duties for half an hour and I went in the stockroom, cleared off a corner of the long work table, and opened the brown paper bag I'd brought from home, taking out a sandwich and an orange. I was pouring hot tea from my thermos when Lee came in the back door of the shop with a sandwich and a can of Coke he'd bought from a vending machine.

"Mind if I join you?" he asked.

"I hope you will," I told him. "I hate to eat alone."

He pulled a wooden crate to the table, upended it, and sat down opposite me. With much tugging, he got the plastic wrap off his sandwich, muttering that whoever packaged it must have planned for it to be put in a time capsule as it certainly wasn't intended to be opened anytime soon.

"But you beat the odds and opened it anyway," I said and laughed.

"Just call me 'Never Say Die Carlyle.' Seriously, Christy, this morning I didn't have a chance to find out anything about you. You go to Greenview High?"

"Yes. I'm a senior."

"Great school. I had fun there. What do you do with your time when you're not in class or working here?"

"Oh, eat and sleep — and study." I had another sip of tea. "We may be living in the nuclear age, but homework goes on forever."

He nodded in agreement. I thought the questions were finished, but I was mistaken.

"In addition to eating, sleeping, and studying," he continued, "do you date?"

That query caught me by surprise. There wasn't any reason for my cheeks to turn rosy, but they did. My, "Of course," seemed to come from deep in my throat.

Lee was fishing for information about me. Since he and Mike knew each other, maybe I should have mentioned Mike's name and said that Mike Maxwell and I were going steady, but the words wouldn't come. I was flustered, anxious for us to get off the subject of me, and to stop his questions I asked about the two-year community college he attended. It was located some ten miles east of Greenview.

"Are your courses interesting?" I said.

"You know how it is, Christy."

"No, I don't . . ."

"Some are, and there are always a few duds."

"Oh, if that's what you mean, I certainly do know. I've never had a year when all my teachers were super."

"I can't say much for my Economics prof, but Math and Biology classes are okay. Next fall I hope to transfer to the University of Virginia — if I can get in there. It's a mammoth 'if' because it probably will depend on how my grades shape up this year. I've been out of school a while and believe me it's tough to try to pick up the habit of studying again. There are a lot of other things I'd rather do at night than hit the books."

It amazed me that Lee and I were chatting as if we'd been friends for a long time. I couldn't believe I was as much at ease with a boy I'd just met as I was with him — and then, I caught myself. Lee Carlyle was at least nineteen or twenty, possibly twenty-one, and scarcely could be classified as a "boy." I didn't feel as relaxed with him as I did with Mike, but I'd only known Lee half a day. At least I wasn't tongue-tied and silent, fighting to say *anything*.

To keep the conversation going, I asked Lee how he'd spent the time since his graduation from high school, recalling vaguely that Mike said something about Lee working for relatives in another state.

Lee took so long to reply I thought he must be ignoring me. He finished his sandwich, crumpled

58

the wrapping, and aimed the wad at a trash can across the stockroom. It bounced off the rim and fell six or seven inches short.

"Missed," he muttered and went to get the paper, deliberately returning to where he'd been sitting on the crate, and tossed the plastic once more. That time it went in the can.

"Bull's-eye," I said. "Score one for you." I made an imaginary check mark in the air.

"Yeah. On the second try. That's the story of my life." He sucked his breath in. "You asked about these last couple of years. I've been in Kentucky. My uncle lives there and raises horses — thoroughbreds. When I was a kid I used to have a great time visiting him and I spent half the summer there between my junior and senior years of high school. Sooooo," he drew the word out, "I talked him into taking me on as an employee after I had my diploma. It seemed like a fantastic setup at the time, but it wasn't the smartest move I ever made."

"Why do you say that?"

Lee gave a short, jerky sigh. "I'm too big physically to be a jockey and I knew it, of course. Figured I'd become an overnight horse trainer or breeder and make a few million dollars before I was twenty-one." His mouth twisted into a mirthless smile. "That just proves how dumb I was. It takes years to be a trainer, and if you go into breeding horses, you need a big pile of cash to make a start, as well as good connections with horse people. I was plain stupid. I thought my uncle would make me an instant partner since he doesn't have any children."

"And he didn't?"

"He nearly fell out of his chair laughing when I mentioned it."

"Lee, how awful! But he gave you a job, didn't he?" I persisted.

"Sure did." He clenched his jaws. "Mucking out stables."

I must have looked blank because Lee explained. "That means cleaning up manure, Christy."

My, "Oh?" was scarcely more than a whisper. His uncle, I decided quickly, must be an ogre.

"I found out in a hurry I didn't want to do that the rest of my life," Lee went on, "even though I stayed in Kentucky until this past summer. I was still mucking out stables and not doing much else, and finally I decided to come home, admit to Dad I wasn't setting the world on fire, and try to get some more education. My uncle actually looked relieved when I told him I was going. I don't suppose I can blame him."

Lee sounded as if what he was saying had been pent up inside him for a long time, and that once he opened up and began to talk about it, the words gushed out. I knew that feeling well because it had happened to me, sometimes when I was talking with my mother, and at other times with Mike. Glancing at Lee, I couldn't tell if he felt better or if he wished he hadn't told me any of it.

I didn't want to cut the conversation short, but it was time for me to go back to work, and I told Lee that.

"Wait a sec, Christy," he said. "If you're not doing anything tonight, how about a movie?"

He was asking me for a date!

I wasn't sure I'd heard him correctly, knowing all the time I'd understood every word! I gave a strangled gasp, and to my consternation, I half-stammered when I replied to him. "Thanks, Lee, but — uh — I already have — uh — plans for tonight." My voice was an octave higher than normal.

"Do you mean you already have a *date* planned for tonight?" he persisted as if it was his business to know.

For a second time in half an hour, I realized I was blushing, and I didn't trust myself to answer him with words. Nodding, I hurried from the stockroom into the shop, wondering why I felt self-conscious all of a sudden. *I really should have told Lee that Mike and I are going steady*, I said to myself.

Since I was Mike's girl, I wouldn't be dating Lee Carlyle. Still, it was very, very nice to have been asked.

As usual, Mike was parked in front of the gift shop at six o'clock that evening, and when I got into the car beside him, two voices from the backseat sang out, "Surprise!"

The unexpected noise made me jump. It was Betsy and Gordon, sitting very close together, smiling and speaking simultaneously.

"Don't they sound just like a couple of old bullfrogs in a pond on a July night?" Mike said to me. "I expect they're harmless, though. Frogs usually are."

"Don't you dare make cracks about us, Mike Maxwell!" Betsy pretended to chastize him. "You won't act so brash when we frogs turn into a prince and a princess."

"A green prince and a greener princess? When will that big event take place?" Mike's grin deepened and he added, "Christy, should you and I sit here and wait until it happens?"

"Not me." I giggled. "Thanks, but no thanks." Turning sideways on the front seat, I glanced behind and said, "What gives with you people?"

It was Gordon who answered. "This afternoon when I was buying gas, I mentioned to Mike that Betsy and I were going to take in the new pizza restaurant tonight, and he said you and he might want to join us. Okay?"

Mike's eyes gave me a silent yes. "Sure," I said. "But I'll need to call home and tell Mama not to count on me for dinner. She's probably ready to put the food on the table right now."

"That's been done," Mike told me as he turned on the car's engine. "I phoned her before the service station closed, but you can do it anyway if you want."

My mother would expect me to call and Mike knew it. After thanking him, I began talking about my day at the shop, on the verge of saying I'd met Lee Carlyle although I had no intention of mentioning Lee's invitation for the movies. But before I uttered Lee's name, Mike cut in to announce that Bud Warren had gone to Richmond.

"Bud's mother wanted to do some Christmas shopping in Richmond so he drove her there today," Mike went on. "They left early this morning and are coming home late tonight."

He must have realized I hadn't finished what I was saying. I began again, commenting that it was the busiest day I'd had since going to work for Mr. Carlyle. This time there was no doubt in my mind about Mike's deliberate interruption. He cut in again, blurting out that it seemed strange not to be heading for Sonny's if we were going anyplace to eat on a Saturday night.

I felt almost as if I'd been ordered to shut up. Biting my lower lip, I was thankful for the darkness in the car as it hid the expression on my face. I knew I must look stunned as well as hurt, and I was angry, too. Mike wasn't a rude person and he wasn't one of those individuals who refuses to let anybody else talk. Now, though, he had stopped me twice, changing the subject, and each time it had happened when I'd been trying to describe my work at the gift shop.

A crazy, nagging notion surfaced in my mind. *Is my job so much more interesting than Mike's that it upsets him to hear about it?* That was hard for me to believe. I decided not to make an issue at the moment, although at some future time I'd ask him about it.

"Every restaurant needs competition and that includes Sonny's," Gordon said, his voice slicing into my thoughts.

"Not Sonny's where hamburgers are concerned," Mike came back. "Sonny's already makes the world's best burgers. Don't you think so, Christy?"

He glanced in my direction as he stopped for a red traffic light, apparently attempting to draw me into the discussion. *Does he realize how rude he's been to interrupt me?*

I murmured, "Yes," to the question about Sonny's hamburgers, then became silent.

Gordon leaned forward from the backseat, his mouth at my ear. "Amen to that," he said. "But tonight I still want to try this pizza place. I go for Italian cooking, and besides, a new eating spot doesn't open in Greenview often. It's a big occasion."

The restaurant was named La Roma and it was located in what formerly had been a dress shop. The tables were covered with red-and-white checked cloths and the walls were decorated with pen-and-ink sketches of Rome, Venice, and Naples. Hanging basket of green plants filled what had once been display windows, and the tangy smell of tomato sauce, herbs, and cheese was everywhere.

We four agreed the pizza was delicious and the prices were reasonable, but that it wouldn't replace Sonny's for us on a permanent basis. Lots of townspeople were eating there, especially teenagers. I recognized Mrs. Holton, my history teacher, who was with a man I assumed to be her husband, and also recognized several boys and girls I knew at school.

In a subconscious way I found myself searching for Jill, hoping she and whoever she was dating would *not* decide to eat pizza and join us, something she'd done other times and which ruined evenings for everybody else. She couldn't have been around because I didn't see her bright hair or hear her laughter.

I saw someone else I knew, though. Lee Carlyle.

As Betsy, Gordon, Mike, and I were leaving, walking across the restaurant parking lot, Lee got out of a sleek red sports car. He was with a girl, a pretty girl as blond as he was, her golden hair spilling over the shoulders of her dark coat.

So he got himself a date, I thought, consumed with curiosity to know when he asked her. Did he make up an excuse for not inviting her sooner? Or maybe he always made his dates at the last minute. He hadn't given me much advance notice, either, but then, he and I had just met. Had Lee phoned the blond girl from the gift shop as soon as I returned to the book section after lunch? While the questions whirled through my brain, I reminded myself sharply that what Lee did wasn't my concern.

The four of us smiled and exchanged hellos with Lee and the girl, but didn't stop. Gordon and Betsy were walking in front of Mike and me, Mike holding my hand the way he always did. I couldn't tell if Lee noticed that, although the parking area was well lighted.

When we were in the car, Betsy said, "I haven't seen Lee Carlyle in ages. I'm sure it's been more than a year. He always was cute enough looking to be a movie star."

"Hold it!" Gordon piped up. "You'd better not spend your time looking at other guys, movie star types or not. I thought we were going steady."

"We are. But a girl can still look, can't she? Anyway, you're cute enough to be a movie star, too. Satisfied now?" Betsy giggled and gave him a light kiss.

I wished Mike could kiss me. It was impossible since he was driving, but I leaned against his shoulder, the rough, tweedy material of his jacket rubbing my cheek.

"Christy, is Lee working for his father at the gift shop?" Betsy asked.

"Yes," I said. "He started today."

Mike stiffened. "Don't tell me Lee is helping you sell paperbacks?" he grunted.

"At times he probably does a little of everything." I fought to hold my voice steady. "Today he was a combination stockroom clerk and janitor."

I hoped that explanation would make Mike relax, but he remained rigid for the next few minutes. His fingers curled around the steering wheel as if he believed the car would fall to pieces if he loosened his grip. He and I were silent, and although I hadn't moved away from him and our legs still touched, I felt as if an invisible barricade was between us.

He's just tired, I told myself, rationalizing. Mike had put in a full day at the service station; most of his time was spent outside at the gas pumps and the weather was freezing. I refused to consider that in all the time Mike and I had been dating, I'd never known him to be sleepy or, if he was, to admit it.

To my relief, Gordon started describing a funny television program he'd seen, and it was impossible not to laugh. When that happened, I glanced at Mike and realized his tension was fading at last. His jaws were no longer clenched, and his body was settling into a natural position in the driver's seat.

Betsy had a suggestion. "Why don't we go to my house and play Monopoly?" she said.

"Sounds good to me," Mike answered. "Okay with you, Christy?"

I said yes, and Gordon agreed. It was something all of us enjoyed. At Betsy's, we put the board on a card table in her den, and the game was wild. Gordon won everything including Park Place and Boardwalk, bankrupting the rest of us.

Two and a half hours later when Mike and I

started to my house, we watched a full moon, almost crimson in color, come over the mountains and grow paler until it was a glowing orange circle as it lifted into the black sky. Lee Carlyle's name wasn't mentioned, and I purposely didn't refer to the gift shop.

The loving good night kisses Mike gave me were proof that whatever had been bothering him earlier was no longer important.

IX

I was ecstatic when my mother asked if I would like to ask Mike to have Thanksgiving dinner with us. I'd been thinking about it, wanting to invite him but a little apprehensive for fear Mama and Dad might feel the holiday should be strictly a family affair, even though there were just three of us in our immediate family and our other relatives lived hundreds of miles away.

Of course, *I* considered Mike one of us, and my parents obviously liked him and always made him welcome, but my mother was big on family traditions for times like Thanksgiving and Christmas. She wanted everything the same year after year on those holidays, the same activities, the same decorations, the same menus. She called that "making our own traditions."

Usually Mike let me out of his car at home after school on Mondays, Tuesdays, and Wednesdays without coming into the house as he had to hurry to his job, but on the Monday afternoon before Thanksgiving, I had a tremendous pile of books from the school library and he helped me carry them from the car. The pungent smell of cinnamon and nutmeg filled the kitchen as we opened the back door. My mother was baking applesauce cookies.

"Here, Mike. Take these with you," Mama said, handing him several cookies in a paper napkin. "You can munch on your way to work."

"Thanks," he answered and bit into one. "Mmmmm — super! And they're still warm. I go for warm cookies. You're the most, Mrs. Jamison."

If Mike and I had been by ourselves, I'd probably have teased him by saying, "I thought I was 'the most,'" but I didn't talk that way in front of my parents. It wasn't that Mama wouldn't have understood, but I was still hesitant to reveal my emotions about a boy. Mike and I were careful not to be too personal unless we were alone.

I watched through the bay window in the kitchen until Mike's car was down the hill, before pouring myself a glass of milk and taking three cookies. Mama took the final pan from the oven, carefully lifting each cookie off with a spatula.

"Christy, it looks as if you tried to check out the entire school library," she said.

"Seems that way, doesn't it?" I eyed the books. "Mrs. Natwick assigned us a paper today and it's due before Christmas vacation begins. I figured I'd better do my research and get my notes in a hurry because I have an idea I'll be at the gift shop lots of afternoons from now on. Mama, did I mention that Mr. Carlyle wants me to work all day Friday of this week since there's no school the day after Thanksgiving?"

"Yes, you told me." She put the cookie sheet in the sink and turned around, looking into my face. "I hope your school work isn't suffering because of this job."

"It isn't. And it won't, Mama. That's a promise."

I finished my snack, brushing cookie crumbs off the table with one hand and letting them fall into my other palm.

"It's just that I'm having to rearrange my study habits," I added. "It used to be that I could do stuff like this history paper on Saturdays because Mike was at the service station and I had all day to myself. Now, though, I plan to cram like mad this afternoon and tonight, and the same tomorrow and Wednesday, but I absolutely refuse to study Thanksgiving Day."

I didn't mention that before the late spring, when I began dating Mike and when I'd had every evening and all day Saturday to study, I'd been miserably lonely.

"Are you and Mike planning something special for Thanksgiving Day?" Mama asked.

"Not really. I just feel holidays should be different from other days."

"Will Mike's brothers be in town, Christy?"

It wasn't like my mother to be so full of questions. "I don't know," I answered. "Mike hasn't said."

He seldom talked about his family and I could understand why. His two brothers were so much older than he that both were grown by the time he entered the first grade. Jack now worked for a building contractor in Pennsylvania and Louis was a career Marine. Mike was lucky if he saw them once a year, and I'd never met either one.

I liked his parents, the little I knew them, although it constantly surprised me that Mike didn't spend much time doing things with them. It wasn't the warm relationship Mama, Dad, and I shared, and sometimes I suspected Mike actually felt closer to his Uncle Eben who owned the service station than he did to his father or mother. His dad worked for a farm equipment firm and Mrs. Maxwell was a secretary at the courthouse several miles from Greenview.

Mama finished putting the freshly baked cookies into a pottery jar and washed her hands. "Christy, if you'd like to have Mike here for Thanksgiving dinner with us —" she began.

I didn't wait for her to finish. "I would!" I burst out.

"Talk about an eager response!" She smiled, "That must have set a record."

I managed a self-conscious laugh. "He's going to phone me between ten and ten-fifteen tonight," I said. "I'll invite him then. And, Mama, it's really great of you."

* * *

Everything was perfect on Thanksgiving Day, but what happened forty-eight hours later on Saturday night spoiled the holiday weekend for me.

For Mike, too, I suppose. It wasn't completely my fault — or his, and there were events we didn't plan or want. Both of us got mad Saturday night, but for different reasons, and we made some hurtful remarks. Maybe we'd had too lovely a time Thursday and by the law of averages should have expected a little unpleasantness, although it seemed trouble was coming at us from many directions, piling up like grains of salt poured in a glass jar.

My mother planned Thanksgiving dinner for two o'clock in the afternoon, reasoning that since nobody in the house had to go to work or to school, we could have a late, light breakfast. "Then, if you want something else after dark, you and Mike can make turkey sandwiches," she told me.

Mike arrived around one and he was wearing a suit, looking, I thought, more handsome than ever. He and Dad sat in the den and talked while I helped Mama in the kitchen with the last-minute things. I stole glances at Mike as we took our seats at the dining room table, hoping he liked sitting across from me as much as I enjoyed watching him. I had on an outfit I didn't wear to school, a mauve tweed skirt and the long-sleeved white silk blouse with tiny pearl buttons which had been a gift from my aunt in Indiana. I didn't know if I actually looked beautiful or if I just felt that way from being happy.

73

Mike and I washed the dishes. He offered — I knew he would because he always did — and when Mama protested that he was in his best clothes, he grinned at her and said, "Guess what, Mrs. Jamison? I came prepared. Brought some jeans. They're in the car."

"Mike, that wasn't too smart!" Dad laughed. "Now you don't have any excuse to avoid doing the dishes."

"It's the least I can do after that dinner. That was the best meal I ever ate, and I've had some really fantastic ones here. About the jeans," he turned from my parents to me, "when I decided to bring them, I had another motive. Christy, I thought you might want to take a walk this afternoon. It's cold but nice. There's no wind."

I nodded, eager to go out of doors. While Mike changed clothes in the downstairs bath, I ran up to my room and got into jeans and a woolly plaid shirt. We made quick work of tidying the kitchen, and when we stepped into the yard, it was the most natural thing in the world for my hand to be in his.

In front of our house, our lane circled up from the highway, while in the back, a series of rolling hills stretched a long distance. By the end of November, the yard was a blend of drab colors, the grays, browns, and smutty blacks of winter showing everywhere. Frost had killed the grass and only a few dead leaves clung to tree branches, the shrubs already taking on a rusty appearance. Yet, the air was clear enough that Thanksgiving afternoon for us to see all five ranges of the Blue Ridge on the horizon.

We strolled across the backyard halfway down the hill to the big rocks where we had sat so many summer evenings to kiss, walking past the spot where my mother planted her garden. Nothing grew there now, and the dead stalks of flowers and vegetables had been cut.

"Christy, remember the day Uncle Eb sent me to plow your mother's garden and you rode on the tractor with me?" he asked, his hand tightening on my fingers.

"I'll never forget. . . ."

Every moment of that Saturday in April was engraved on my memory. I'd been embarrassed to see Mike that afternoon because some weeks earlier he'd asked me out, but had never tried to date me again. One date and no more was a horrible embarrassment. My mother must have known how humiliated I felt although she never mentioned it to me, and I was too hurt to discuss it with her or anyone else.

Yet, I was still drawn to Mike. Being near him at school was agony and not being near him was worse.

When Eben Maxwell found a man to plow Mama's garden, and the man didn't show up to do the job, Mr. Maxwell sent Mike who brought a small tractor on a tow chain attached to the back of the service station truck. Mike was half-finished

75

plowing when Mama made me take a can of Coke to him, and she became exasperated with me because I didn't take a can for myself.

"Christy, when I was your age I was shy, too, just as shy with boys as I could be," she'd said, handing me a second Coke. "I didn't know then that boys feel the same way, even the ones who seem very sure of themselves. If Mike doesn't want to drink the Coke or if he's in too big a rush to talk a few minutes, you'll know it. But give him a chance. At least have a Coke for yourself just in case."

It took all my courage to carry the two cans of Coke down the hill to where Mike was riding the tractor. I honestly thought I would be ignored, that Mike didn't want anything to do with a girl who couldn't keep a conversation going, but he seemed glad to see me. We chatted and he asked if I'd like to ride the tractor with him, and I did, sitting with him on the bucket seat with my back against his chest, his arms on either side of me to keep me from falling off. Dust swirled around us and I hadn't minded grit in my throat or getting dirty or the rough bounces. I'd felt his laughter before I heard it, felt it rumbling deep inside his body, and in spite of my precarious perch, I felt safe with him.

On Thanksgiving afternoon, remembering the tractor ride, April seemed a long time in the past, and I said that to Mike, seeing him nod. We continued to stroll, reaching the bottom of the hill and starting up the next one, crossing a meadow and stopping by a patch of woods where the earth was covered with layers of brown pine needles.

"Mike, do you remember the first time you kissed me?" I asked softly.

"Sure. Now that you've brought the subject up, I could kiss you right here with a little encouragement on your part."

It was fun to flirt with him and make silly remarks. "What sort of encouragement do you mean?" I asked with pretended innocence, leaning toward him, my hands flat on his chest.

The laughter in his eyes was replaced with tenderness as he put both his arms around me and pulled me close. His lips were firm and cold from the chilly air, and very, very sweet.

On the day following Thanksgiving I mentioned to Mike that Christmas Eve wouldn't be any more frantic in the gift shop than that Friday had been. The store was jammed with customers on Saturday also, and by the end of each afternoon, fatigue had put an ache between my shoulder blades and my smile felt as artificial as a mannequin's. I enjoyed the work, but a breather would have been welcome. There was scarcely time to bolt my sandwich at noon, and conversations with Lee consisted of one or two hurried sentences when he brought books from the stockroom or pitched in to help wait on customers.

The two days after Thanksgiving were just as rough for Mike. "I think everybody in this town suddenly decided to have cars repaired," he said to me. "Uncle Eb had to turn some of them away. Told them to come back the first of the week, so, I guess we'll have another rush then."

Friday night he and I were content to stay at my house and watch a TV movie, and we watched television a short time again on Saturday night, although the programs didn't hold our interest. Another four-way Monopoly game might have been fun, but Betsy was in Maryland visiting her grandmother and Gordon had just started a Saturday job at one of the supermarkets and would work late. Around nine-thirty I could sense that Mike was becoming restless, and it didn't surprise me when he suggested our going to Sonny's.

Every small town probably has a place where teenagers gather to eat and gab. In Greenview, people of all ages went to Sonny's during the day, but at night, mostly high school and college students were there. It wasn't glamorous as the front section was a narrow, rectangular room with a soda fountain along the left wall and a row of high-backed booths on the right. In the rear, past a latticed arch entwined with green plastic vines, all of it made to resemble a garden trellis, the second room was square, with tables and chairs.

When my family first moved to Greenview I'd learned quickly from conversations at school that certain unwritten standards existed for teenagers about going to Sonny's. Mostly, dating couples went, or a boy could go by himself with no eyebrows raised and sometimes two or three girls went there together, but for some ridiculous reason a high school girl didn't go to Sonny's alone. I didn't go until Mike took me in the spring, although since then, I'd been many times with him.

The booths in the front section were filled on the Saturday night after Thanksgiving. Mike and I nodded to people we knew and headed through the arch to the back, finding that room almost as crowded. Each table had six chairs, and I didn't see a completely empty table although several had some vacant seats.

"Hey! Maxwell! Over here!" Bud Warren said from behind us.

I recognized his voice, Mike and I turning at the same instant to see Bud and Jill Rogers alone at a table against the wall. There was no way we could avoid joining them.

My mouth went dry, every nerve in my body suddenly taut. Sitting with Bud was all right, but being with Mike's former girl even for a short time made my knees shaky, and the warm smile she turned on Mike melted my self-confidence. *She still wants to date Mike*, I thought.

"Any action on these premises tonight?" Mike asked as we took chairs at their table.

"Lots of people but no excitement," Bud came back.

"That could change now that you two are here," Jill said, her eyes on Mike.

She said *you two*, but she ignored me. Her hair was a glowing copper circle around her face and as much as I disliked her, I had to admit to myself that she was beautiful.

"Are you just sitting, not eating?" Mike inquired.

He addressed the question to Bud, but it was Jill who answered, saying they'd arrived only a moment before we did. "Bud," she added, "I'd like a lemonade with lots of ice."

Mike glanced at me, waiting for my order, and because I had to say something, I mumbled that I'd have lemonade, too.

"No burger, Christy?" he asked and I shook my head. Ten minutes earlier when we were in his car, both of us admitted to being hungry, but my appetite had vanished at the sight of Jill.

Sonny's didn't have table service and when the boys went to the soda fountain for the food, Jill and I were alone. She hummed softly, her eyes roving around the room, the corners of her mouth turning up into a smile. I wondered if she was deliberately ignoring me and if she knew how frantically my heart was beating and how much I was trying to think of something impersonal to say. She didn't care any more for me than I did for her. I realized that instinctively.

In desperation, I mentioned school. We talked briefly about the history paper due before Christmas, becoming silent again. She continued to hum, glancing everywhere as though she was trying to find someone more interesting than I was.

I can't explain what happened next except that I was thinking about her and Carl Browning and remembering how she looked on the back of his motorcycle the Fourth of July. To my surprise, I heard myself ask her about him.

"Carl and I date occasionally. Nothing heavy," she answered in a flippant tone.

"Oh?" It was a lame reply, but she was staring at me as if she expected me to speak.

"Carl's in Washington this weekend for a football game," she went on. "Two pro teams are playing. Why do you ask, Christy? Are you interested in dating Carl? I can put in a good word for you with him if you want."

"No! *No!*" I gasped, my cheeks burning. "I just asked."

If she told Mike I'd asked about Carl Browning, I knew I'd be uneasy. Carl wasn't important to me. I was merely trying to keep a conversation going.

"Look, there's Lee Carlyle!" she exclaimed and waved to him, calling in a loud voice, "Come on over, Lee."

Lee, who was with the blond girl he'd taken to the pizza restaurant, started in our direction, inching between the chairs. I don't think he noticed me until he'd almost reached our table as my back was toward him, and his, "Hello, Jill," was followed by a warm, "Oh, hello, Christy. How are you? I see you survived the stampede at the shop this afternoon."

Maybe Jill had forgotten I was working for Lee's father, if she ever knew it, because she looked surprised and for just a moment, I thought I saw annoyance in her face. That expression vanished quickly. Lee's date was Maureen Graham, a student at the community college, and while I was acknowledging the introduction, Mike and Bud came through the latticed arch with our food. They seemed to be laughing at some joke and weren't looking at the table. Bud, his protruding ears giving him a perpetually funny appearance, didn't appear to be upset at the sight of the two newcomers, but Mike's face hardened.

The evening fell apart — for me, anyway.

After a few minutes of general chitchat, Lee began teasing me about trivial incidents at the gift shop, and when he explained to the others what he was talking about, everybody chuckled — except Mike. Jill cut in, changing the subject, asking Lee about the time he'd spent in Kentucky, flirting openly with him, which annoyed Bud. I felt sorry for Maureen who was left out since the other five people knew each other. I'd been in that position enough times to know how awkward she must feel, and I tried to talk to her but didn't get much response. All that time Mike was eating his hamburger and French fries in silence and when he finished, he said, "Christy, don't you think we should be hitting the road?"

"What's your hurry?" Bud asked.

Mike ignored the question, his eyes moving swiftly around the table. "See you folks later," he said. "Good to have met you, Maureen."

He glanced expectantly toward me and I got to my feet, ready to leave although it seemed impolite to be abrupt. Still, it was easier to go than to irritate him by lingering, and I was more than ready to get away from Jill.

Outside, the night air was raw. Mike and I

didn't say a word to each other until we were in his car. I couldn't decide if he was angry with me or irked that Lee and Maureen had joined us, or maybe, he wasn't at ease with Jill now that his romance with her was over. The idea was wishful thinking and I knew it.

I looked at him. His face seemed to be carved from stone.

"Mike, aren't you going to turn on the heater?" I asked, shivering.

Reaching to the dashboard, he flipped a switch which brought a blast of icy air and I shivered again, thankful a minute later when it was followed by warmth.

Greenview streets were deserted and many of the houses we passed were dark. Mike didn't appear to be in a hurry in spite of the urgency he'd showed in leaving Sonny's, and he didn't act as though he realized I was beside him. He hadn't touched my hand or put his arm around me as he usually did when we were in the car by ourselves. I looked at the six or eight inches of space between us and thought about sliding over nearer to him, but couldn't bring myself to do it. Then, I wanted to ask him what was wrong, and didn't do that, either.

As we drove through town I drew a deep breath and decided it would be better to just have a casual discussion and give him a chance to unwind. The remarks I made were wrong, though. I wondered aloud if Greenview people had completed the bulk of their Christmas shopping and if business at the gift shop would be lighter during December.

"Please don't get off on that subject again, Christy," he growled. "Okay?"

His voice was rough and I recoiled, feeling almost as if I'd been slapped.

"Get off on what?" I said.

"That darned job of yours! It's just temporary work, not a career! You act like you're president of the world because you're working for Sam Carlyle!"

I turned my head, staring at him after that outburst. His profile was a silhouette with his jaw firm and his shoulders squared. I was hurt and angry and troubled, all the emotions mixed up inside me to form a lump in the bottom of my stomach.

"Am I boring you, Mike?" I asked stiffly.

"How would you like me to yak all the time about Uncle Eb's service station? I could mention how many gas tanks I filled or who got a lube job or that I changed four tires today and only two yesterday. Big deal, isn't it? About as big a deal as your selling umpteen books and then making change for the customers!"

Twisting my body around, I gazed through the car window, not seeing anything through the tears in my eyes. Mike's harsh retort stung and I blinked frantically, determined not to cry in front of him. But he must have realized how ugly he sounded because he apologized.

"Christy, I — uh — didn't mean to — to blow off," he muttered.

84

At any other time I'd have inched over to him and rested my cheek against his shoulder, whispering that everything was all right. It wasn't all right, though. I didn't move.

The silence in the car was a barricade between us. When I couldn't endure it any longer, I said, "Both of us could use some sleep," and my voice seemed to belong to another person.

The silence remained until he braked beside my house. At night my parents left porch lights burning at the back and front entrances if I went out, and in the past Mike and I had joked about walking a short distance into the yard to have privacy for saying good night. That Saturday night, without discussing it, we went straight to the door.

"I'll call you in the morning," he said. Phoning Sunday morning was as much a routine for us as brushing teeth.

I was angry about the things he'd said in the car, and I heard myself answer, "Better make it afternoon, Mike. I have lots of homework and I'd like to finish the rough draft of that History paper. I really should study most of tomorrow."

His, "Okay," had a choppy sound.

We faced each other. I didn't think I could live if he went home without kissing me even though at that instant, I wasn't sure I could return a kiss. Instead of the warm embrace we normally exchanged, he leaned forward a little and so did I, our lips barely brushing together. It was five minutes to eleven and on Saturdays Mike always stayed later, but he didn't suggest coming in and I didn't invite him. I wanted to do it but something held me back, a nameless something. Maybe fear had a lot to do with it. I couldn't bear to ask him and have him refuse.

Inside the house, I paused to steady myself, not wanting to have to talk to my parents but aware that if I didn't speak to them, my mother probably would follow me upstairs to make sure I wasn't sick. They were in the den, Mama reading and Dad deep in a crossword puzzle. Dance music, soft and melodic, came from the radio and they looked so happy and comfortable that the turmoil in me increased because they were at peace and I wasn't.

"Good night," I told them. "Mike and I are tired so he went home early."

Their answering good nights echoed as I ran to my room.

The remainder of the night was terrible. I was too keyed up to get to sleep at once, and after tossing restlessly for more than an hour, I got up, wide-eyed, and without turning on a light, wrapped a blanket around myself and sat on the window seat in my room. Mama and Dad had long since gone to bed. I'd heard them come up the steps, moving quietly so as not to wake me since they thought I was asleep.

Wind rattled the tree branches and the night coldness made the old house settle and creak as if ghosts were walking in the attic. The landscape beyond the bay window was shadowy, the starless sky a peculiar yellowish gray like a thick curtain which blotted out any sight of the mountains. I drew my knees under my chin, hugging them with both arms, wishing my mind would stop churning.

Something was wrong between Mike and me, and I didn't know what it was or what to do about it. He still cared for me. I felt sure he did — almost sure. And I still loved him. I knew that positively.

This was our first real fight although it wasn't *actually* a fight — at least, I didn't think it was. But if we fell into the habit of bickering or making hurtful remarks or if we lost the wonderful closeness we'd shared all summer and autumn, we wouldn't want to continue dating. The prospect made me shiver and I clutched the cover tightly around myself, but the chill in my body wasn't one which could be changed with blankets.

I don't know how long I sat huddled on the window seat, going over and over every moment of Saturday evening in my mind, silently repeating what Mike and I said to each other, what we said to the people at Sonny's, and how they replied. Did Mike truly resent my job? Could he possibly be jealous of Lee simply because Lee and I worked together? Would Mike be jealous of any boy — man — I worked with? Was Mike falling out of love with me and into love with Jill again and didn't know how to break the news to me?

I had no answers to those questions.

After a while, I crawled into bed again. Finally, once I was warm, I slept.

* . * . *

Sunday morning I awakened to find myself half off the bed. I had been dreaming but couldn't remember anything about it once I'd opened my eyes, although I knew Mike was part of the dream. Conscious of a vaguely dissatisfied feeling, I looked at my watch to discover it was a quarter after eleven, much later than I usually slept when I didn't have to go to work or to school. As I sat up and fumbled on the floor for my bedroom slippers, all the questions and problems of Saturday night came surging back.

Snow was falling but not sticking, the wet flakes melting as soon as they hit a surface. I put on a housecoat and went downstairs to find that Dad had driven into town to buy a newspaper. My mother was seated at the kitchen table, writing a letter to Aunt Doris who lived in Indiana.

"Good morning." Mama smiled at me. "Want some breakfast?"

Telling her truthfully that I wasn't particularly hungry, I dropped a slice of bread in the toaster and poured a glass of orange juice. My mother had an uncanny way of sensing when I had something on my mind, and she was silent as she finished her letter, folded the three sheets of paper and slipped them into an envelope. I brought my toast and juice to the table, sitting opposite her, conscious that she was watching me without being obvious about it.

As I met her eyes, I felt myself crumple inside.

"Mike and I had a fight last night," I blurted out. It took all my willpower not to sob.

"Did you make up before he went home?" she asked.

"Sort of." I lifted the glass of juice and returned it to the table without taking a sip. "Not really," I admitted brokenly. "Mama, I'm not even sure what we were fighting about."

"You aren't the first person ever to feel that way." She gave a twisted smile. "It isn't always easy to point to the cause of a quarrel, but the important thing is to make peace as soon as you can. The longer you wait, the harder it will be."

I kept quiet because I didn't trust my voice. Under the rim of the table, my hands were trembling.

"Christy, surely you have some idea of what's wrong between you and Mike, don't you?" she said.

"He — he gets tense if I mention the gift shop. Do you think it could be my job? At first, he seemed to think it was fine for me to work there, but now . . . I'm not sure . . ."

"Well, lately that job of yours has been your primary topic of conversation. That's understandable."

"Do you mean I bore you talking about my job?"

My mother gave me a straightforward answer. I knew she would whether it was what I wanted to hear or not. "It's fascinating to me," she said slowly as if she was choosing her words with care. "But Mike seems to resent it. This is something he's not directly involved with, and in a subconscious way he could hate the thought of your doing something you enjoy if he isn't part of it. He wouldn't want to work in a gift shop any more than you'd want his job at the service station, although he may not think of it in those terms."

My hands became fists. "But he acts almost jealous, Mama!"

"Perhaps he is . . . a little."

"But I —"

The telephone interrupted me. She got up to answer it.

"For you, Christy," she said. "It's Mike."

I felt myself shaking as I put the phone to my ear. After being so sure of Mike ever since the August night in the hospital when he told the nurse I was his girl, suddenly I was afraid of what I was about to hear him say.

My, "Hello," was barely louder than a whisper.

"Christy," his voice seemed choked, "I'm sorry about last night. I don't know what happened after we left Sonny's and I shouldn't have said what I did to you. I could see you were upset, and I'm sorry." He cleared his throat. "You told me not to call until late this afternoon, but I can't wait that long."

"I'm glad you didn't wait, Mike. I've been so miserable."

"Me, too. Are you still mad?"

"No. Are you?"

"Mad with myself, Christy. Not with you. Look, I have a pile of homework and you said you did, too. What if I bring my books over in a little while and we study together?"

I felt as if a heavy weight had been taken off my body.

"I'd like that, Mike," I told him. "Let's forget about last night and never mention it again."

"Suits me. See you soon. Is half an hour from now too quick?"

"Half an hour is lovely. I can't wait."

Closing my eyes for a moment, I realized I was smiling as I turned away from the phone. I wasn't conscious of anything except feeling good again, and I'd forgotten my mother until she spoke.

She hadn't hovered over me while I was talking to Mike, but she must have heard my end of the conversation. "I take it everything is fine between you two now," she said, smiling.

"Oh, yes! Mike has been just as upset as I was."

"And he's coming here in a little while?"

I said yes. "He's welcome to stay for lunch," she went on.

"Thanks, Mama. I'd like that."

"Christy, I don't mean to butt in, but I couldn't help hearing you tell Mike something about never mentioning the argument again. That might not be wise."

"What do you mean?"

"Wouldn't it be better to bring everything out in the open now that neither of you is angry? If you don't do it quickly, sometime you could have that same quarrel again. I'm speaking from experience because that has happened to me."

"I don't want to talk about last night and Mike doesn't, either," I told her emphatically. "Mama, please don't let Mike know I said anything about it to you."

She nodded, and I knew she could be trusted. All of a sudden, the gray morning wasn't drab any longer and the fat snowflakes were attractive instead of merely being wet globs as they melted on the windowpane. There were wings on my feet as I raced upstairs to have a bath and get dressed.

X

On Monday morning Mike was waiting in his customary spot at school when I got off the bus, the collar of his jacket turned up around his neck and the familiar black knitted cap pulled low over his ears. It was bitterly cold with the sky gray enough to give a hint of bad weather to come, but in spite of snow falling most of Sunday, there wasn't any accumulation except on the north side of the school building where the frozen ground was streaked white.

Mike reached for my hand and we hurried inside. "It's not much warmer in here than it was outside," I commented as we hurried along the corridor to our lockers.

"The thermostat is turned down during weekends to save fuel," he said. "Give it another hour and you'll be sweating from the heat."

I tossed him a smile. "My Aunt Doris says men and horses sweat. Girls and women perspire."

"Is that right?" He grinned. "She's a regular

walking encyclopedia, I take it. Bet you can hardly wait to see if you perspire or sweat so you'll know which you are."

We laughed as we separated to go to our homerooms. "See you later," I said, glad things were back to normal between us. Just as we planned over the phone Sunday morning, we hadn't discussed our Saturday night disagreement.

The building remained cold and in second-period class I noticed several girls had been to their lockers to get coats. My slacks and bulky cardigan weren't heavy enough to keep me comfortable and my hands were so numb that writing was an ordeal. Other students were having the same problem, and ballpoint pens and pencils constantly slipped from stiff fingers to the floor.

The announcement came over the intercom into each classroom at the end of third period. Mr. Brady, the principal, began by saying he realized we were thoroughly chilled.

"So am I," he continued. "This building is twenty-nine years old and we're still using the original heating system. *Were* using it until today. The furnace reached the point of no return this morning. Two engineers and an architect have taken a look at the situation as has Mr. Matthews, head of maintenance for the county school system, and it is the opinion of these knowledgeable people that we have done all the patching we can do on our present furnace.

"They recommend installation of a completely new heating system and estimate it will require about three weeks to get the equipment and install it. The school board has been meeting in an emergency session for the past hour, and the decision has been made to close Greenview High School today and not reopen it until we have an operating furnace."

A cheer went up in my class. Maybe students in other rooms had similar reactions because Mr. Brady said, "Now, before you become overly excited at the thought of an extended winter vacation, let me remind you that under the laws of this state, schools have to operate one hundred eighty days a term, and if we miss any of those days, the class time must be made up."

For a split second there was silence in the room. Mr. Brady coughed and the intercom crackled.

"The other schools in the county system will continue on the regular schedule and take holidays of one week before Christmas and one week after," he said. "Students and teachers at Greenview High will return to school on the twenty-sixth of December, granting that we have heat by that time as we expect, and the other missed days will be made up by having classes on Saturdays throughout January and February."

The cheers were replaced with collective groans.

"But I have a job on Saturdays!" a boy's voice rang out from the back of the room. He sounded distraught.

"Nobody's going to make me go to school Saturdays," Anita Winfield, who sat across the aisle from me, hissed. "My family takes ski trips nearly every weekend from Christmas until spring and I don't intend to miss the fun."

Miss Laurens, the teacher, held up her hand for silence as Mr. Brady began to speak again.

"The school board is aware that these arrangements will be unpopular," he said. "They know it will be a hardship for some of you, but it appears to be the best way of handling an unfortunate situation. A few students may have legitimate reasons for not attending Saturday classes and their requests will be handled on an individual basis after Christmas.

"On the other hand, if there are students who decide simply to stay away from school these Saturdays in January and February, be advised right now that unexcused absences will count against your semester grades, and if you should chalk up enough unexcused absences, it might result in your receiving F's."

He concluded by telling us that wishing the student body Merry Christmas the first week in December was somewhat premature, but added that he was doing it anyway. "There will be a short faculty meeting in the auditorium in fifteen minutes," he said. "Students are dismissed now."

It seemed to me there was more muttering than rejoicing as we poured out of classrooms. The prospect of a dreary January and February took away excitement over the unexpected three-week pre-Christmas vacation.

When I stepped outside the building, Mike was

standing beside his car in the parking lot, his breath making pale curls of steam in the icy air. He had the engine running.

"This sure isn't a typical Monday, is it?" he asked as I approached. "What do you want to do with what's left of the day?"

"Get warm." I managed a shivering smile.

"Amen to that. I guess the motor has been on long enough now for the heater to function."

It wasn't actually comfortable in his automobile, but it was better than being in the cold school building. "Uncle Eb will expect me at the station at the regular time this afternoon," Mike went on, "but for now, want to go some place and grab lunch?"

I nodded, making a mental note to phone home. Mama would be interested in hearing about the school situation.

"And after lunch, what about you?" Mike asked. "I'll drive you to your house or drop you off anyplace you want."

My chills weren't quite as acute with hot air from the car heater blowing against my body, but Mike's question made me apprehensive. There was no way to avoid mentioning the gift shop if I replied honestly to him.

"Mr. Carlyle may want me to work more now that I don't have to go to school," I said. "After lunch I think I'll stop by the shop and ask him."

Keeping my eyes focused straight ahead, I stared through the windshield because if the reference to my job irked Mike, I didn't want to watch his good mood change. He turned on the radio and drove out of the parking lot, apparently concentrating on traffic since the buses were leaving and so were other students who'd come to school in cars. When I finally glanced at him, no tension showed in his features. I exhaled slowly, relieved that we were avoiding another crisis.

We went to Sonny's and joined Betsy and Gordon who were alone in one of the front booths. Everything seemed easy and natural between Mike and me, and he didn't utter a word about my job, not even when I announced after phoning home that Mama said Mr. Carlyle had heard about the school furnace and had already called the house to leave a message that he would like to have me full-time at the shop until Christmas.

XI

It seemed odd to be going to work instead of to school Tuesday and I had the same strange feeling Wednesday and Thursday mornings. Not having homework to do at night was heavenly, though, and when I commented about it to Mike, he agreed, saying he felt as if he was out of jail. He'd already told me his uncle seemed glad to have him at the service station all day.

"Right now Uncle Eb has more business than he can handle, but that won't be true forever," Mike said. "He doesn't want to break in a new employee for a short time and maybe have to let him go later."

"Mike, you and I are fortunate to have jobs. Betsy can't find anything although she thinks she might be hired to answer the phone in a beauty shop the week before Christmas."

He picked up my hand, lacing his fingers between mine. "Bud can't find a job, either," he said. "Bud hoped the ice cream plant would need him since he worked there all summer and knows the ropes, but the boss said nix. I don't suppose people eat as much ice cream in winter as they do in hot weather. Gordon isn't overly keen about the supermarket, but at least it gives him a paycheck."

Thursday morning there were so few customers in the gift shop I had plenty of time to straighten up shelves in the book section. Mrs. Gibson, who was doing the same thing with bric-a-brac, china, and crystal, remarked that she had an idea we'd see some slack days after so many sales during November.

"Just you wait, Christy," she added. "If this week is down, next week will be terrific. I've worked for Mr. Carlyle eight years and it happens like this every Christmas."

That Thursday Betsy came in the shop to buy a book on flower arranging for her mother, and I decided my mother might enjoy owning that same book so I put a copy aside. A world atlas would make a good Christmas gift for Dad, and I'd get a discount on anything I bought from the shop. I realized I'd have to do some thinking about Mike's present. He enjoyed reading but wasn't as interested in books as my parents.

Two girls I knew slightly at school came in to buy paperbacks and a gray-haired lady almost cleaned out our supply of picture books, after telling me she had four grandchildren and two great-nephews under school age. As soon as she left, I went to the stockroom to let Lee know I needed more picture books in a hurry.

Lee had been in and out of the shop all morning, bringing new merchandise, pausing to chat if I wasn't with a customer, making silly cracks which had me smiling. I hadn't seen him the two previous days and when I asked if he was sick, Mr. Carlyle explained that Lee's exams had started. The community college, which operated on the quarter system instead of semesters as the high school did, closed Wednesday afternoon for a long winter break and wouldn't reopen until early in January.

When Lee brought me a load of picture books Thursday morning, I mentioned those examinations. "So you'll go back to new classes and the start of a new term after Christmas," I said. "Lucky you. I dread returning to exams."

"I know what you mean, Christy. In case you're interested, I got my grades late yesterday and I passed everything, which came as a shock since I'd been out of school such a long time. I'd braced myself to flunk at least one course. Hey —" he looked at me and grinned, "passing everything ought to call for some kind of a celebration."

"Fireworks and marching bands, to say the least," I came back.

"Naturally. But they aren't enough. Anybody

101

can have fireworks and marching bands, but we ought to have trained monkeys and you might toss in some dancing girls riding elephants, along with other assorted goodies." Still grinning, he disappeared into the stockroom once more.

Shortly before noon Lee came to the book department again. He had taken off the khaki coveralls he usually wore when he was opening crates and was in jeans with a wheat-colored shirt which accented his tawny hair.

"Christy, let's go somewhere for lunch," he said. "This can sub for that celebration we were discussing, because I don't think we're going to locate any elephants or trained monkeys today."

It was fun to kid with him. "But what about the sixteen brass bands I've lined up?" I asked.

"Only sixteen, huh? I was hoping for a better turnout than that."

Both of us laughed. "Thanks Lee, but I can't leave the shop long enough to go out and eat even though we don't have many customers at the moment," I told him reluctantly. "My lunch break is just half an hour."

"I've cleared it with Dad, so, put on your coat. He'll look after your section and he won't go bananas if we're a few secs past half an hour coming back. And by the way, don't offer another excuse and say you brought a sandwich from home."

"I did bring one."

"I figured. Save it and we'll split it this afternoon for a snack. Right now, though, I'm not in the mood for a stockroom meal."

Lee didn't ask where I' like to go and I took it for granted he was taking me across the street to a quick food restaurant where he and his father often ate lunch. Instead, we went to Sonny's and I tensed as we walked into the soda shop because it was my first time there without Mike. There was no reason for me to feel nervous, but I did, and I hoped Lee wouldn't notice. We were slightly ahead of the usual lunch crowd, early enough to get one of the booths.

Mike told me once that those booths originally were in a drug store which had gone out of business when the owner died. Everybody preferred the booths to the tables in Sonny's back room, and I did, too, which was strange as the booths weren't especially comfortable and they certainly weren't attractive, but they did afford a little privacy for conversation. The tall-backed wooden seats were painted a rusty brown and the rectangular tables were topped with what looked like marble, the white stone flecked with veins of gray and all of it covered with scratched initials and scribblings. Despite the fact that the surface was too hard for carving with a knife, determined students had discovered over the years that filling deep scratches with ballpoint ink served the same purpose.

Lee and I decided on chili and grilled cheese sandwiches, a good wintertime menu, and he went to the soda fountain for our food. As he returned and took a seat opposite me, I saw Bud Warren coming through the door, and my throat muscles tightened. Bud glanced around as if he was trying to spot somebody he knew, and his eyes met mine, his forehead wrinkling in surprise. I knew what he was thinking; he was amazed to see me in Sonny's with any boy except Mike.

"Hi, Christy, Lee," Bud said and walked past us without stopping.

When I attempted to reply, I couldn't make a sound. *If Bud tells Mike he saw me eating lunch with Lee Carlyle* . . . I couldn't finish the thought, but the possibility of another unpleasant scene with Mike made me very tense.

"Something the matter with your food, Christy?" Lee asked. "You aren't eating."

"I — uh — I'm waiting for the chili to cool." It was the first excuse I could think of, and it was valid as steam was rising from the bowls. Picking up the sandwich, I made myself taste it, the melted cheese a burning glob on my tongue.

Suddenly, I came to my senses. I wasn't *dating* Lee Carlyle. We were friends and nothing more. As soon as I saw Mike, I'd mention having lunch with Lee at Sonny's, and meanwhile, all I could do was hope Bud wouldn't have any reason to go to the service station during the afternoon and tell Mike before I had a chance to do it.

It was pitch dark when I left the gift shop at six o'clock and the wind was gusty. A blue pickup truck was parked in Mike's usual place near the shop but I glanced down the street and recognized his car at the corner.

As I walked in that direction I reminded myself to be casual when I said something about lunch. "Guess where I ate today?" I'd comment, and when Mike said, "Where?" I would answer, "Sonny's," adding that the chili was delicious once it was cool enough to eat and that Lee had it, too. I would say quickly that I'd seen Bud at Sonny's and ask if Bud was having any luck locating a job for the holidays. If I didn't give Mike an opportunity to get a word in, and if I could start him talking about Bud — or about anything else — he might not make an issue of my lunch with —

The thoughts about lunch died. I gave an involuntary gasp and stopped in my tracks some twenty or thirty feet behind Mike's car.

Mike hadn't seen me because he hadn't been watching for me to leave the shop, and the reason was obvious. Somebody was in the automobile with him, and there was no doubt about the identity of that person. Jill Rogers. The street light shone on her bright coppery hair and the tinkling laughter could not belong to anyone except her.

I had to will myself to move to the car. Mike and Jill saw me at the same moment, both of them saying, "Hi, Christy," as if they were two puppets programmed by a computer to act in unison. I think I spoke. I tried to do it, but with such a roaring in my ears, it was impossible to hear my own voice.

I went to the passenger side of the car just as I always did, and instead of getting out to let me sit next to Mike, Jill scooted over to the middle of the front seat which put me next to the door with her between us.

Jill, her leg pressed against Mike's, began to bubble.

"Mike saw me walking home and offered me a ride and am I ever glad!" She gave me a quick glance and immediately turned to Mike. "Isn't it great to be out of school? Oh, all of us will detest Saturday classes after Christmas, but for the present, I love the vacation. This will be one year I can do my Christmas shopping early. Mike, did I tell you I had a letter from Vince Halloran the other day? He's still in Ohio, working in a quick food place now because he was laid off from his job in a plant that manufactures kitchen appliances . . ."

Jill rattled on with Mike making occasional murmuring comments. I said nothing. It was all I could do to breathe. Mike was enjoying her chatter. I knew it by the way he smiled.

At her house, he got out of the car and she slid under the steering wheel.

"Good-bye for now, Mike," she said, her eyes on him. "Thanks a million for the ride."

"Anytime," he answered.

He gave me a puzzled look as he got in the car once more. I saw it from the corners of my eyes and I didn't move, my side pressed against the door with enough space between us on the front seat for another person to sit comfortably. When he braked at an intersection, I knew he was looking at me once more. I could feel his eyes, but I managed to continue staring straight ahead although I wasn't seeing anything through the glass.

"No need for you to act so weird, Christy," he said finally.

"Weird?" My voice was dry. "I don't know what you mean. I don't think I'm weird."

"You could sure fool me, the way you're clamming up."

"I'm not rude enough to interrupt when other people are talking and that's the only way anyone else can say something when *she's* around!"

I didn't mean to sound so hateful or to refer to Jill, but I'd done it, and that was all Mike needed.

"Jill was going home from downtown when she saw me and stopped by the car to say hello." He swerved around a corner a lot faster than usual. "She said she needed a ride and, after all, it was dark. It's not smart for a girl to walk around alone at night."

I bit my tongue to keep from spouting what I was thinking. Jill must have guessed Mike would be parked near the gift shop at that hour, waiting for me. If he hadn't been available to drive her, she would have walked home by herself in spite of the cold and the darkness, wouldn't she? Jill wasn't going steady now and while she might date Carl Browning and various other guys, apparently she'd like a serious romance. Bud adored her but she used him, only dating him if she had nothing more interesting lined up, and as for Vince, who had been her steady before he dropped out of school and went to Ohio, her remarks about his

107

letter didn't indicate that he had plans to return to Greenview in the near future.

She had been Mike's girl after Vince left town and she was still Mike's girl at the time I moved to Virginia. Although I didn't know her true feelings about Mike, whether or not she cared for him as deeply as I did, I was positive of one thing: she would like to be his girl again.

My anger toward her gnawed at me, and it was jumbled up with fear as I sat in Mike's car with all that space between us. I wanted to inch over nearer him in the car, to reach out and touch his face, to hold his hand . . .

But I couldn't. I couldn't do it because Jill Rogers was there with us just as much as when she actually sat between us on the front seat of the automobile. I could sense her presence, even smell her perfume.

Mike turned off the highway and drove the car up the hill to my house. Beams of light came through the first floor bay windows, splashing yellow rectangles into the yard. The lump in my throat was tremendous. There was so much I ached to say to him, and I couldn't speak.

"Christy, are you giving me the silent treatment because I offered Jill a lift home?" he snapped, anger making his voice rough. "Just because you and I are going steady, you don't own me! I can still talk to other people! Come to think of it, I've known Jill a hell of a lot longer than I've known you! Where is it written that I can't give a friend a ride?"

I felt myself shrivel. Opening my mouth, I closed it in silence. Mike had never spoken to me that way and if I'd answered him, I would have burst out crying. I couldn't sit there indefinitely so I got out of the car because I didn't know what else to do.

Pausing to give him the chance to say something which would make things right between us, I waited for him to tell me what time he'd be over later, which was what he did every evening. He didn't say a word. Raising my eyes, I forced myself to look at him, and he appeared to be gazing at something off in the distance, his jaw thrust out and his hands clutching the steering wheel. He hadn't cut off the car engine and the hum of the motor was the only sound in the still night.

Twisting around, I ran into the house and straight to my room. Without turning on a light, I stood by the window in the darkness and watched his car disappear. He was going very fast as if he couldn't wait to put miles between us, and the tears I'd been holding back rolled down my cheeks.

"Christy, is that you?" my mother called from the foot of the stairs. "I thought I heard you come in."

When I didn't answer because my voice seemed to be frozen, I heard her coming to the second floor. I was still at the window and I was crying hard.

"Christy, what —" She touched the light switch. I averted my face and tried to will myself to stop weeping. Mama realized I was crying, of course, and she crossed the room to me.

"What's wrong?" she asked.

"I — Mike — W–We had a fight . . ."

She said all the things I knew she would say . . . soothing statements . . . it would blow over . . . by tomorrow it would be forgotten. It must have taken a lot of self-control on her part not to remind me she'd suggested that Mike and I bring our differences out in the open after the other disagreement.

"Everything is wrong," I whispered brokenly. "Everything."

"Do you want to talk about it, Christy?"

"I — I don't know." I drew a shuddering breath. "Mike doesn't love me anymore."

It took her a long time to speak. Maybe the silence only lasted a few seconds, but it seemed like an hour to me until she said, "Did Mike tell you he didn't love you?"

"No. Not in words. But — But . . . I know."

She slipped her arm around my shoulders. "You're tired from working all day and I'm sure Mike must be just as worn out as you are. He'll go home and eat dinner and feel better, and food will help you, too."

"Mama, it's not that simple."

"I'm sure it isn't. But standing here isn't going to help. I want you to wash your face and come downstairs."

"I'm not hungry."

"You can eat a little, Christy. At least, you can try. Moping like this won't help and if you continue to cry, you'll have a headache. Your daddy is already home, taking a nap in the den, and I was waiting for you to get here before waking him and putting dinner on the table."

My mother thought a cold washcloth and some food would solve all the world's problems. The idea might have seemed comical to me if I hadn't been so upset. When she left I went to the bathroom and held a cold cloth to my eyes, but I purposely didn't glance in the mirror.

The pulse in my temples pounded and my chest felt as if it was weighted down with a huge rock. All that time I prayed silently that Mike would phone me the second he reached home, knowing he'd already had plenty of time to do it, but hadn't called.

The meal was a horrible experience. Mama must have told Dad that Mike and I had a quarrel because he didn't ask questions although he must have noticed I'd been crying. Some girls look sweet and arouse sympathy when they sob, but I wasn't one of them. My eyes always swelled and turned red, and my cheeks looked blotchy. I had deliberately avoided seeing my reflection in the mirrror, but I knew how awful I must appear.

Dad and Mama talked about everything — except about Mike and me. I attempted to take a few mouthfuls, each bite growing harder to manage. In desperation I dropped my fork on the plate and ran upstairs.

Mike will phone soon, I told myself. *He will. I know he will.*

This time, *I* would apologize before he had time to do it. When he called or came over, I'd say I was sorry, and maybe we could forget this latest trouble as we'd practically forgotten his irritation about my job.

Maybe. . . .

An hour later my mother came to my room. "You're sitting here in the dark again," she chided and turned on the bedside lamp.

I was on the window seat. Whenever a car came into view on the highway, I caught my breath, hoping desperately the automobile would turn into our lane and that it would be Mike, but the cars continued to whiz past. None of them slowed or turned.

"Why don't you come downstairs and watch television with your dad and me?" Mama asked. "You'll feel better if you get your mind on something else."

"I'm all right," I mumbled without moving.

"Listen to me, Christy." She sat down at the other end of the window seat. "All people who have a close relationship disagree at times. Your daddy and I do, but we don't nurse grudges and we try to talk our problems out. We make it a point to get back on good terms before bedtime because if you go to sleep angry, you'll wake up with that same feeling. You —"

"Just leave me alone for now," I interrupted

her. "Please, Mama. I know you're trying to help, but — but —" I didn't finish the sentence.

With a sigh, she started for the door, one of her hands lingering on the knob, and I had the feeling she couldn't decide whether to rejoin Dad or stay with me. I was afraid she might order me to follow her to the den and sit in front of the TV set, but she didn't.

The silence in my room was eerie. I continued to look through the bay window for the car which didn't come, seeing headlights flash — as traffic moved around the curve on the road — and then disappear quickly. By ten o'clock the waiting was too painful to endure and I crossed the hall to my parents' room where the extension phone was located. I couldn't endure the agony of not speaking to Mike any longer.

The minute I dialed the Maxwells' number I began to burn up and freeze at the same time. The phone rang once, twice, three times, four, and I'd almost given up hope by the time his mother answered on the fifth ring.

"This is Christy Jamison," I said and my voice squeaked. "May I speak to Mike?"

"He isn't here, Christy. I haven't seen him since breakfast. Is there a message?"

Pressing the phone against my ear, I managed to say, "No, Mrs. Maxwell. Thanks," and I hung up. There were a million messages I wanted to leave, but I couldn't put them into words.

Mike hadn't gone home after he'd left me at my

house almost four hours earlier. *Is he at Jill's?* The question was a knife jabbing into my heart.

I buried my face in my hands and stumbled back across the hall to my room.

XII

The gray morning matched my mood. I choked
down part of a glass of juice and a little scrambled egg so my parents wouldn't comment on my
not eating, but I couldn't make myself touch
bacon or toast. Mama drove me into town that
Friday just as she'd done every day since school
closed, both of us quiet until she pulled up in
front of the gift shop.

"Wait a minute, Christy," she said as I started
to leave the car. "I know you're upset, but remember that while you're working you need to
push your personal problems aside. Mr. Carlyle is
paying you to serve his customers, and you should
make yourself present a smile to the public. Nobody likes a grumpy salesperson."

Some smile, I thought, my mouth twisting.
When I'd looked in the mirror while I was comb-
ing my hair, my face resembled a gruesome Hal-
loween mask and the lack of sleep showed. There

were circles under my eyes and my mouth drooped.

Aloud, I thanked Mama for reminding me. I knew she was right. "I'll try," I told her, avoiding her eyes.

Business in the shop that Friday was steady without becoming hectic since the rain, which started at midmorning, probably kept some customers at home. Lee wasn't around, and I asked Mrs. Gibson about him when I needed a new supply of how-to books on home repairs.

"Mr. Carlyle said Lee is helping some friends move today," she answered. "He might come in later. I don't envy him — or the friends he's helping. This really is terrible weather for moving."

At noon I found the crate of how-to books, carried an armload to the book section, and then ate lunch by myself in the stockroom. Or rather, I tried to eat, pinching off tiny bits of sandwich and forcing down a third of a cup of hot tea, halfway wishing Lee would pop in because chatting with him might have taken my thoughts away from Mike. But in another sense, I was glad not to have to talk to anyone since I needed time alone to plan what I'd say to Mike when he came for me at six o'clock.

I was going to apologize to him. That much was for sure. But all the blame wasn't mine for the angry words we'd exchanged and I wanted him to realize he'd hurt me. If anything I said during the apology made his conscience bother him, good enough. He'd caused me pain, and he had never returned my phone call. True, I hadn't left a message for him to do it, but surely his mother mentioned that I was trying to reach him.

During the final minutes of my brief lunch break I considered phoning Betsy. She might have seen Mike, or if Gordon had, he probably would have mentioned the fact to her.

I couldn't do it, though. What happened between Mike and me was very, very personal. I couldn't bear to talk about the fight, not until Mike and I made peace. *If* we made peace. That *if* was a hurting word.

The gift shop was ready to close for the day when Lee arrived. He was a mess, the legs of his khaki coveralls were spattered with mud and there was a long gray smudge on his chin. His hair, usually neatly combed, was tousled with a water-sprinkled cobweb resting on the top of his head, and his hands were absolutely grimy.

"Oh, boy, do I need a shower!" He grinned by way of a greeting. "I just stopped here at the shop to find out if Dad has any dirty work he wants me to do before I go home and clean up. We had a freight shipment today, but he said to hold it until tomorrow morning. Moving sure is one messy deal even though the two guys I helped don't have much furniture."

"You don't have to draw me a picture about moving," I said, forcing a weak smile. "My father's company has transferred us so many times I dread even passing a moving van on the highway.

There's no easy way to pack and unpack a household without feeling like you're up to your elbows in dust." I smiled again — or tried to — aware that my facial muscles were stiff.

"Did I miss any excitement in the shop today?" he asked.

"Nothing. It was strictly routine."

My coat was buttoned and I felt in the pockets for my gloves, wishing Lee and I could continue talking but it was five minutes past six and I wanted to hurry to Mike.

"See you tomorrow, Lee," I said and went outside.

A cold, drizzling rain was falling from the overcast sky with the pavement shining wetly. Very little traffic was in evidence and only two cars were parked on the block and the few people walking seemed eager to get to wherever they were heading. I pulled the hood of my coat up to cover my hair and looked in every direction for Mike.

A feeling of panic rose into my chest. *Mike wouldn't do this*, I thought desperately. *He wouldn't let me stand on the street in the rain and the dark . . . waiting . . .*

I stayed in that one spot for another three or four minutes with the rain dampening my face and my coat, my hands and feet so cold they were clumps of ice. Mike wasn't coming. I knew he wasn't. Finally, fighting desperation, I did the only thing I could do and went into the shop again.

Lee was turning out the lights and Mr. Carlyle

was talking on the phone in the rear of the shop, his voice echoing in the silent store. Lee gave me a surprised glance.

"Thought you'd left," he said.

"I need to call Mama or Dad to come for me."

"Christy, I'll drive you home. That is," Lee's mouth widened into a grin, "if you don't mind the way I look."

I murmured a grateful, "Thanks," adding, "There's nothing wrong with your looks that a little soap and hot water won't change." It amazed me that I was able to make a casual comment like that when so many emotions were putting me into a state of inner turmoil, but I didn't want Lee to know I was troubled.

His red sports car was newer and fancier than Mike's ancient sedan. I started to give him directions to my house but he shushed me with the statement that he already knew where I lived, and if I hadn't had so much on my mind, I'd have asked how he knew. The moment for the question passed.

Lee did most of the talking, telling me the two fellows he helped move were Sandy Rexford and Dave Freeman, that they were long-time friends, and now were his classmates at the community college. I didn't know either of them as they had graduated from Greenview High before I came to Virginia, but I had heard their names.

"They did what I did after high school and goofed off a while before they came back to Greenview and decided to go to college," he continued. "Since September both of them have been living with their families, but they wanted to get living quarters somewhere else, only they had to wait until they could find a cheap apartment."

"And they finally found one?" I inquired.

"Located it this week. Sandy works at the new pizza restaurant five nights a week and Dave has a job after classes at his father's hardware store. The apartment is nothing special and it's furnished in Early Attic, but —"

"Early Attic?" I broke in, puzzled.

"That's how I classify their furniture," Lee chuckled. "It's stuff they scrounged from their parents. The furniture isn't exactly an interior decorator's dream. That's why I'm so filthy, Christy, from shoving junk around in two attics. The Freemans must have saved every cracked dish, scrap of paper, and broken chair since World War II, and the Rexfords were just as bad. I've never seen so much worthless trash. So, you see why I term it Early Attic."

The explanation made me laugh, and something happened to me with that laugh. I relaxed a little and part of my desolation ebbed away. The twitch in my stomach stopped and my head no longer felt as if a tight rubber band was squeezing my forehead.

"Christy, Dave and Sandy are having a party tonight to celebrate being in the apartment," Lee said as he drove up the hill to my house. "How about coming with me? I'd better warn you that it won't be a fancy shindig, just sort of a get-together."

He braked at my front steps. The porch light illuminated the interior of the car and for an agonizing moment I hesitated, my mind spinning as I tried to make a decision. I looked everywhere but at him. It was flattering to realize a college man was interested enough in me to include me at a party with his friends, and I genuinely liked Lee. Yet, there was Mike . . .

The windshield wipers swished back and forth. I peered past them at the rain, watching the drops flatten out on the car's hood and fenders. *Why should I endure another bleak, lonely evening when I could be having a marvelous time?* Being miserable was no fun, and I'd had my fill of it. *Who needs Mike Maxwell, anyway?* I asked myself, dumbfounded to realize I wasn't as much on the defensive about Mike in my thoughts as I'd been a short time earlier.

Thinking those questions made my decision. "I'd like to go with you tonight," I told Lee in a voice which was amazingly steady considering the way my heart pounded against my ribs.

"Good. See you at eight-thirty, Christy. Don't dress up. Jeans probably will be the uniform of the night."

I tried to reply but found it was easier to settle for a smile as I stepped to the ground.

His car was a red streak going down the hill.

As I let myself into the house Mama called

instantly from the kitchen. "Christy, is that you?" she asked as she always did. She obviously had been watching for me or listening for the sound of an automobile. I answered yes, hung my coat in the hall closet, and joined her.

She was standing at the sink washing a head of lettuce, tearing the crinkled green leaves apart and holding them under the cold water faucet before laying them on paper towels to drain. The kitchen seemed unusually bright and welcoming. Veal chops sizzled in the frying pan on the stove and the spicy scent of apples flavored with cinnamon came from the oven. Until that second I wasn't conscious of being hungry, but all of a sudden I felt starved. In the past twenty-four hours I'd eaten practically nothing.

"Is it still raining?" my mother asked in a studiedly casual tone.

"Yes, it is. Dinner smells yummy."

"I hope it will taste yummy. Did Mike bring you home tonight?"

She spoke in the same too-casual tone she'd just used to inquire about the weather. Sucking my breath in, I focused my gaze on the African violet plant blooming on the kitchen windowsill because I didn't want to look at her.

"Lee Carlyle brought me." The words tumbled out and I said the rest of it quickly. "Lee has invited me to go to a party tonight." I was panting as if I'd been running.

Mama didn't speak at once. She continued to wash lettuce, carefully shaking each leaf to remove excess water until the last one was finished, and then, she turned to me. She wanted me to tell her more about the party and about Lee — and about Mike. I knew it as clearly as if she'd said it aloud.

The cooking chops gave off a faint hissing sound. I couldn't stare indefinitely at the tiny purple flowers on the violet plant or at the lettuce, and when I made myself meet her eyes, her face was filled with unasked questions.

My cheeks felt strangely hot while the rest of me was chilled. My tongue seemed to be pasted to the roof of my mouth. I wanted to tell her all of it, and I couldn't. Not yet. Maybe someday I would, but not that evening. My feelings weren't completely sorted out and I wasn't able to talk about Mike, not to her or to anybody.

"I'll set the table," I murmured and crossed the kitchen to take cups and saucers from a cabinet.

"Where is this party, Christy?"

"At the apartment of some friends of Lee's."

I didn't tell her whose apartment. "He didn't give me the street address," I added quickly. "It's in Greenview, not out in the county."

The china felt cold and my fingers tightened around the plates as I set them on the table. The way Mama slid her tongue over her lips made me believe more questions about Lee and the party were forthcoming, but I was mistaken. Going to the stove, she lifted the pan of apples from the oven, and the cinnamon smell grew stronger in the room.

"Don't be later than midnight coming home," she said.

"I won't."

To my relief, she changed the subject. "Christy, please fill the salt shaker, the one on the table. I noticed at breakfast it was almost empty. You know how much it irritates your father to have us constantly jumping up when we're eating."

XIII

Lee arrived looking freshly scrubbed, his jeans and dark green sweater showing under his raincoat. I'd followed his suggestion and also put on jeans with a tailored white blouse and a pale blue cardigan.

I took him into the den to meet Mama and Dad because in my family, it is unheard of not to introduce a friend. Dad stood up and stretched out his hand to shake Lee's, and my mother laid her book in her lap, giving him a lovely smile as she said she was happy to know him. One thing I could always count on was that my parents would be cordial to anyone who visited me. That night they probably were overflowing with questions about why I was with Lee Carlyle instead of Mike and I didn't doubt they wanted more information about Lee, but they gave no indication of asking.

The rain had slowed to a damp mist although water continued to drip from soggy tree branches. Lee had a green plant in a brown clay pot, a six-pack of beer, and a six-pack of Cokes in the car, and as soon as I was seated, he put the plant in my lap.

"Do you mind holding it so the pot won't topple over, Christy?" he asked.

"Of course not."

"That plant is an apartment-warming gift for Dave and Sandy. My mother has so many plants at our house she doesn't mind getting rid of one." He gestured to the cans. "This party tonight is a bring-your-own drinks affair. The beer's for me, and I'll share it with you if you want, but I figured Cokes might be your preference. Am I right?"

"Yes. Thanks, Lee."

I clutched the plant firmly as he guided the red car around the curve on the hill. Just to be saying something, I commented, "You must have taken the world's most thorough bath and used a full bottle of shampoo, not to mention an entire cake of soap."

He took his eyes off the road for a brief second and winked at me. "Do you mean I look better now than I did late this afternoon, Christy? Aw, come on . . ."

"You certainly do," I assured him, laughing.

"Thanks for noticing."

"How could I help noticing?" I smiled again.

"I doubt if I ever looked any more cruddy than I did when I brought you home after work. I didn't realize it was quite that bad until I went home and Mom made me undress in the utility room so I could dump my clothes in the washing machine without tracking dirt all over the house."

126

His grin broadened. "It's a good thing I didn't meet your folks before I had a chance to clean up or your dad might not have let you go out with me. Did you get a load of the cobwebs I was carrying around on the top of my head this afternoon?"

"Did I ever?" I came back and laughed. "I thought you were trying to launch a new type of hairdo."

Conversation with Lee was so easy I felt as if he and I had known each other for ages. The evening, I decided silently as I steadied the plant on my knees, was going to be Fun with a capital F. I determinedly put everything out of my thoughts except the great time I'd have with Lee and his friends.

Later, though, thinking back about all of it and going over everything in my mind, I realized that fun, whether it began with a capital letter or not, wasn't the proper word to describe the events of that night. Not for me, anyway.

At first, I enjoyed myself, and nothing really *bad* happened, but I wasn't prepared for what took place or how I reacted. I guess I thought I'd feel at ease the entire time I was with Lee's friends, and it wasn't quite that way. Maybe surprising would have been a more appropriate term for the party than fun.

Lee drove almost all the way through Greenview, past the gift shop and the high school, to an old brick house on the outskirts of town, a dwelling which must have been an elegant home at one time but which now had a ramshackle appearance. It was set in a grove of trees a short distance off the street, and as we turned into the driveway and proceeded to an area which had been cleared for a parking lot, the car's headlights illuminated the front of the house. Paint was peeling off the white columns supporting the porch roof and the sagging steps were between unpruned tangles of shrubs.

My mother and I had noticed the house in the past and commented to each other several times that it was a shame to see an old mansion fall into such a sad state of disrepair. Lee hadn't mentioned the actual address to me in advance and I'd had no idea where he was heading, but I realized Mama would be interested when I told her I'd seen the inside of that house. The place had been converted into a number of apartments, and Lee said his friends lived on the third floor.

"Going in the back way and using the fire escape to get upstairs is quicker since the guys' apartment faces the back," he said as he cut off the car's motor. "But the front looks better. I'll take you in through the front door if you want so you can see the big hall and the circular stairs. It looks as if it could have come straight from *Gone with the Wind*. Originally, the house belonged to the Holt family and I suppose it was a real showplace years ago, but most of the Holts died and the others moved away and the property has been sold several times just since I was a kid. None of the recent owners apparently wanted to spend what it would cost to put it in tiptop condition again."

"I do want to see it," I told Lee. "Old houses are fascinating. At least, I think they are now, but I didn't feel like that until my family moved to Virginia and into a Victorian house with nine bay windows."

Crazy windows, Mike had called those bays the first time I met him. He'd asked where I lived and I had explained that Dad bought the "old Toscin house" a couple of miles out of town. Mike promptly gave a mischievous grin and answered, "Sure, I know where it is. It's the house with all those crazy windows."

Walking beside Lee Carlyle to the house which had once belonged to a family named Holt, I caught my breath and attempted to will myself not to think about Mike. That was almost as futile as ordering my heart to cease beating or commanding my eyelids never to blink again.

Lee and I entered a huge hall which was dimly lighted, climbed the wide, curving stairs, and then took another flight of steps, narrower and steeper, from the second to the third floor. None of the halls we passed had any furniture or pictures, although I noticed gray outlines on the dingy plaster where pictures must have hung at one time, and we didn't see a soul despite hearing voices and laughter echoing faintly. Thin slivers of light showed under some of the closed doors.

"Here we are," Lee announced.

He knocked on a paneled door made out of

wood stained a dark walnut color. We waited, and he knocked again. Another half-minute went by and he tried the knob, opening the door without waiting any longer for someone to let us in.

We were in a rectangular living room where a dozen or so people were congregated and it wasn't surprising that Lee's knock hadn't been heard as everyone seemed to be talking at once and the stereo was sending out a loud blast of music. Lee introduced me, taking my hand as we moved around the room. Other couples came in soon after we arrived, and I soon gave up on last names, concentrating instead on trying to match first names with faces. It wasn't easy. Lee's voice was barely audible above the racket even though he was practically shouting.

The only person I'd met before was Maureen, the blond girl who had been with Lee at the pizza restaurant and at Sonny's. She was with a boy named Hal whose left foot was in a plaster cast, and her hello to me was cool enough to make me wonder if she could have forgotten seeing me those other two times or if she resented my being Lee's date for the evening.

I liked Sandy Rexford and Dave Freeman on sight. Dave, short and chunky with reddish hair, had a square-shaped face and a winsome smile. Something about Sandy made me think of Mike, my heartbeats quickening. It wasn't that Sandy's and Mike's features were identical, because they weren't — actually, they weren't especially similar — but both were tall with dark brown hair and smoky blue eyes. Mike's teeth were whiter and straighter, I reflected to myself, and Mike carried himself more erectly. Mike's smile was warmer, too. There were laugh lines at the corners of his eyes and his left eyebrow would lift ever so slightly when he teased me.

Stop thinking about Mike Maxwell. I gave myself that order and tried to listen to what Dave was saying to me.

"Christy, would you like a tour of the apartment?" Dave asked.

"Of course," I answered, wondering what he meant by "tour." Lee had already said it consisted of one bedroom, the bath, and kitchen in addition to the living room.

"The ten-cent tour? Nope." Replying to his own question, Dave looked at me and pretended to be very serious. "Lee said you had to take care of the plant while you two rode over here, so I think you should rate the twenty-five-cent tour. That's the one we classify as a scenic goody. It includes a view of the broom closet."

I giggled and nodded. Still acting as if he was participating in a complicated journey, he said, "Come along. You're in for the treat of your life."

Lee hadn't exaggerated when he called the furnishings Early Attic. I'd already seen the living room with the ceiling sloping under roof eaves and with its battered sofa and assortment of chairs and tables. The green plant was in a place of honor on the coffee table which was made from a sheet of plywood set on cinder blocks, the plant resting beside some thirty-five or forty ashtrays from a variety of restaurants and motels.

Sandy, it seemed, collected ashtrays and his friends picked up whatever they could when they were away from Greenview.

Dave led me through the apartment. The tiny kitchen was next to the bath, and the bedroom, the largest room, was square with a single bed and a studio couch against one wall, while two bureaus and a ten-speed bicycle sat against the opposite wall. Books, mostly college textbooks, were stacked on the floor, and skis were propped in one of the corners.

I'd never been in a boy's room or a boy's apartment before, and since I didn't have any brothers, I was curious. I'm not sure what I expected, but it dawned on me that boys lived differently from girls. Girls who shared living quarters would have made them more personal. Pictures on the walls, curtains on the windows, and the like.

"That's the tour," Dave said. "Was it worth a quarter?"

"Oh, worth twice that much," I laughed. "It really was a scenic goody. Now, if I can just find my purse . . ." I knew it was under my coat which, along with other wraps, had been dropped in a pile on the studio couch in the bedroom.

"You can settle up later," he said quickly, and we laughed again.

The gathering was informal and everybody milled about the entire apartment with most of the conversation having to do with college activities, parties, or sports. Lee had gravitated to one corner of the bedroom to talk to a girl named Amy. She was gorgeous with a perfect complexion, honey-colored hair, and a figure like a model's, and I'd noticed he greeted her with a lot of enthusiasm.

I wasn't really ill at ease, but I wasn't comfortable, either. After a while I was conscious of feeling like an outsider, the way I'd felt when my family first moved to Greenview, and I smiled a lot without saying much. The others didn't appear to realize I was in the room, and once when I peeped into the bedroom where plenty of people were, Lee was still engrossed in whatever Amy was telling him, the two of them sitting on the floor near the ten-speed bike. I made myself circulate, hoping to find a conversation I could participate in, my smile becoming increasingly artificial until my lips felt stretched like an old rubber band.

After a while I found myself next to Hal, who had propped his broken foot on a chair. Maureen was chatting with someone else, and just to be speaking, I remarked to Hal that I knew how miserable a cast was as I'd broken my arm at the end of the summer.

"How did you do that?" he asked and gave me such a penetrating stare I almost had the feeling he'd just seen me, that he didn't recall our being introduced.

"My mother and I were in an automobile accident," I said. "We were on our way to Roanoke when it happened last August. How did you hurt your foot?"

"I should make up a good yarn and claim it was on a ski trip to the Bavarian Alps or that I was in Mexico digging in Aztec ruins." He gave a one-sided smile. "But the truth is that I slipped on a cake of soap in the shower. I guess I'm lucky that a foot was all I broke."

"A cast on your foot must be worse than one on your arm," I told him. "How much longer will you wear it?"

"Three weeks and two days. It itches like crazy, too." Leaning back in his chair, he let his eyes sweep over me in a way that made me uneasy. "Christy — that's your name, isn't it? I don't believe I've seen you before tonight. Where do you go to college?"

There was no cause for me to be embarrassed, but I felt juvenile at having to admit the truth because I knew from overhearing remarks he'd made to other people that he was a junior at the University of Virginia. My tongue was thick as I answered, "I go to Greenview High."

"Greenview High?"

Hal said those two words in such a loud voice that the chatter in the room stopped and, every head turned in his direction. I was standing next to him which meant all those eyes were focused on me, too, and I could feel my face burn.

"Christy, do you mean you're not out of high school yet?" Hal went on and he made it an accusation as if I'd been caught in the act of committing a crime.

"Good grief! Lee Carlyle is a cradle-robber!" a guy named Duncan said from behind us, and everybody laughed.

Some of the people who'd been in the bedroom

returned to the living room to see why there was so much laughter, and I saw Lee with Amy.

"What's the matter, Lee?" an unfamiliar voice said jokingly. "Watch out, everybody! We may have a dirty old man in our midst!"

They probably meant no harm, but the laughter hurt. I was frustrated, wishing I was anywhere on earth except in that apartment surrounded by people I'd just met and, at that moment, didn't care if I never saw again. Lots of laughter followed the comment about Lee being a dirty old man and I overheard a few mutterings which I tried to ignore.

My face had to be turning more scarlet by the second, and that caused new amusement to the boys. I didn't know what the girls were thinking. For me, it was a special agonizing embarrassment to be the center of attention and teased like that whether the cracks were made in fun or not.

"Would you look at the child," Duncan announced, shaking his head at me. "Darned if she's not blushing. I believe that blush is the real thing, too. I didn't know girls did that anymore."

"Cool it, you guys," Lee said, crossing the living room to stand beside me. He didn't touch me or take my hand, and I'd have liked him to reach out.

"Christy, pay no attention to these creepy characters," Lee went on. "Don't let them upset you."

I managed to mumble that I wasn't upset which had to be the lie of the century. The room had become silent enough for me to be heard by everybody, and my voice squeaked the way it always did when I was nervous or troubled, a Minnie Mouse voice. The smile I attempted to force didn't feel at all like a smile, and my stomach seemed to be loaded with chunks of heavy metal.

A beefy boy, one I hadn't met although I'd heard him called Pluto by some of the others at the party, stepped up to me and put his arm around my shoulders, his fingers beating a staccato rhythm on my upper arm.

"Now I know why Carlyle is robbing the cradle," Pluto announced to nobody in particular although he spoke loudly enough to get the attention of the crowd.

"Why?" came a voice amid some laughter.

"Babies are cuddly, aren't they?" Pluto's arm tightened. "Real cuddly. What's your name? Did I hear somebody call you Chrissie?"

I didn't correct him about my name. With my cheeks still burning, I slipped out from under his heavy arm, moving so quickly it must have taken him by surprise, and that meant getting away from Lee at the same time. Inching through the throng to the far wall, I pressed my back against the smooth surface. The apartment was jammed, but all of a sudden I was by myself and that kind of aloneness was an aching pain.

At least I was no longer the center of attention. Conversations and laughter began again, the big group breaking up into smaller ones. Lee, I noticed out of the corner of my eyes, gravitated toward Amy. She had been chatting with Sandy while Lee was rescuing me, if rescue was the correct term, and Lee hooked his arm through hers, taking her out of the living room without even glancing in my direction.

Maureen had taken a seat on the arm of Hal's chair, which didn't concern me as I vowed to myself not to talk to Hal anymore during the evening if I could avoid it. Hal had started the unpleasant scene by making an issue of my still being in high school. Sandy vanished into the rear of the apartment after Amy left him to go somewhere with Lee, and Dave was holding both hands of a cute redhead whose name was Lori. The others were in twosomes or groups. Everybody seemed to have someone to talk to. Except me.

Maybe it was silly for me to feel out of place, but I did. It wasn't my fault I was just seventeen. Most of the people at the party, I'd already discovered, were in their early twenties, all of them juniors or seniors in college except for Lee, Dave, and Sandy who didn't begin college immediately after they were graduated from high school.

I couldn't participate in their talk about college, and it was apparent they weren't interested in hearing about high school. Remaining completely silent would make me appear very dumb, and I didn't want Lee's friends to think he was dating a clod for the evening.

The party stretched out endlessly. Lee mingled. He was no longer with Amy — or I didn't think he was — and he seemed anxious to talk with everyone. He'd grin at me and say, "Having fun, Christy?" when he was near me, and each time I nodded. Finally, I found a seat, the smile on my face as plastic as the chair I was on. I managed a comment now and then, never saying more than, "Yes," and, "No," or, "How about that!" I doubt if it would have mattered if I'd said the house was on fire as my remarks were lost amid the noise.

I hoped it wouldn't be necessary to tell Lee about my curfew, especially after the cradle-robbing jokes, and since he and I had to be at the gift shop by nine o'clock the following morning, I waited for him to suggest our leaving the party before midnight. It didn't happen. No one else left, and I realized many of the others must have jobs, too.

At quarter to twelve I slipped out of the living room to look for Lee, finding him in the kitchen where he was discussing basketball with Sandy. He was sitting on the counter, swinging his feet, while Sandy leaned against the refrigerator, both of them pausing when I appeared.

"Lee, it's getting late," I said.

He glanced at his watch. "But it's not even midnight, Christy!"

"Maybe she has a curfew, Lee," Sandy murmured.

"Do you?" Lee's eyebrows went up so swiftly I realized the possibility hadn't occurred to him.

"Yes. Midnight." I was blushing again. "I — I'm sorry."

"Okay, we'll hit the road." He jumped down off the counter and I let my breath out quickly, thankful he wasn't making waves about going home while the party was in full swing.

We used the fire escape and didn't bother to say good-bye to anybody except Sandy. Lee would be missed eventually, I found myself thinking, but I wouldn't be.

Outside, the cold air felt good to my flaming face, but the rest of me was chilled as we walked across the frozen ground. As soon as we were in the car, Lee apologized for his friends.

"I hope you didn't take offense, Christy," he said. "The fellows were just kidding although they came on a little strong, especially Pluto. Those cracks were aimed more at me than at you, so don't let them get under your skin."

"It's all right. I know what they said about cradle-robbing was — was just in fun. Their idea of fun, not mine," I added.

"I'm sorry." He accelerated and passed a slow-moving truck. "The guys should have shut up when your face turned red. If they'd had any sense they'd have seen you were embarrassed."

In the dark car, my cheeks felt warm and rosy again. "I wish I hadn't blushed," I sighed.

"Don't worry about it, Christy. Blushing probably isn't the worst thing you'll ever do in your life."

He was trying to make me feel better, and not succeeding too well. A memory came rushing back to me, the memory of the day I blushed in the school cafeteria with everybody at the table laughing at me — except Mike. Afterward, I'd confided to Mike that it was humiliating to blush so easily, and a tender expression had come over his face. "I like it, so don't ever stop blushing," Mike had whispered, and I'd been comforted.

Lee's brusk, "Don't worry about it," didn't help much. With a great effort I tried to force Mike out of my thoughts. Sitting beside one boy wasn't the time to think about another.

We left Greenview town limits behind, Lee increasing speed once we were on the highway. My house came into sight, a tall sentinel on the very top of the hill with lights glowing from the first floor windows as well as by the front and back entrances. My parents wanted to make sure no one was hiding in the shrubbery, ready to pounce on my date and me. Mike thought it was a wise precaution although he always grumbled that the lights made him have to plan our good night kisses so we wouldn't be in view. He and I usually walked a short distance into the yard for a tender embrace.

Lee's voice jerked me away from the memory of Mike.

"Does your family own the power company?" Lee muttered. "Or do they just love to use electricity?"

Not knowing how to answer, I let the questions go by. Lee might have gotten a chuckle out of Mike's comments about the lights, but I wouldn't have mentioned Mike to him for the world, much less repeated something Mike had said.

. "I enjoyed the party tonight," I told him. "Thanks for including me."

Without uttering a word, Lee braked, cut off the ignition, and instantly reached out to pull me against his body so swiftly that I gasped. I hadn't expected that, or what followed. His mouth came down hard on mine and there was unveiled passion in his kisses.

His kisses didn't move me at all. Startled, I opened my eyes while his mouth was still pressed to mine — something which had never happened when Mike and I were kissing — and I had the strange sensation of seeing a lock of Lee's yellow hair fall over his forehead. Enough light from the house came into the car for me to see all his features clearly, even to make out the tiny golden hairs of his lashes, but the wild thoughts flowing through my brain weren't about him, but about how wonderful it would have felt to be in Mike's arms with Mike's familiar lips kissing me.

Lee moved his head ever so slightly, putting an inch of space between us. His arms still encircled me although not as tightly as they had a moment earlier, and when he opened his eyes at last, they had a dreamy, glazed look.

I managed to get my palms flat on his chest and I tried to push away from him. His embrace tightened again.

"I — I have to go in," I stammered.

"No, Christy! Not yet —"

"I have to!" It was a stark whisper.

That time I pushed very hard and broke the embrace, fumbling for the door handle and getting

141

out of the car before he could kiss me again. My knees were so wobbly it was necessary for me to stand perfectly still three or four seconds.

Lee got out, too, coming around the car and walking up the front steps of the house with me. The porch light bulb was so large that the area by the door seemed as bright as noon sunshine would have been and, for once, I was glad. I couldn't believe Lee would attempt more kisses under the glare of that light, and he didn't.

It wasn't that his kisses were repulsive. They weren't. I simply didn't want to kiss him or have him kiss me — and I wasn't sure why.

"Thanks for everything," I said softly. "See you at the gift shop in the morning."

"Good night, Christy."

He seemed on the verge of adding something else, but I went inside without giving him the chance.

In the hall I waited briefly until my breathing slowed to normal. The sound of Lee's car grew fainter and fainter until it disappeared completely.

Mama and Dad seldom waited downstairs for me if I was out with Mike, although they'd done it when he and I first began dating. Now, I heard TV voices and knew my parents were in the den and that there was no way I could avoid speaking to them. I steeled myself, hoping it wouldn't be necessary to answer many questions even though Mama, especially, would want to know about the party. It wasn't just curiosity on her part. She was genuinely interested in everything I did.

"Sorry I'm slightly late," I said from the den doorway. My watch showed nine minutes past twelve.

"You're okay." Dad grinned. "You aren't late enough to need an Act of Congress to keep you out of jail."

"How was the party, Christy?" Mama asked. Just as I anticipated, she wanted to know.

"Nice. Lee was right when he said it wouldn't be fancy. It was very informal." Holding one hand over my mouth to stifle a yawn, I added, "I guess I'll say good night because I don't want to fall asleep tomorrow while I'm waiting on a customer."

Saying it was past her bedtime, too, my mother closed her book and put it in a basket beside her chair. I wondered how she and Dad would react if they knew I'd been the only high school student at the party.

There was no need to mention it, I decided quickly. My parents had liked Lee when I introduced him to them. If they hadn't, I'd have sensed their feelings, and I didn't want to do or say anything which might make them veto my dating Lee again. *If* he asked me for another date. Even though he hadn't paid much attention to me at the party, I still wanted to see him again.

Perhaps he wouldn't. The fact that his friends made such a big deal out of his bringing a high school student to the party might make him decide to stick to girls his own age in the future, and my stopping his kisses could have turned him away from me. The strange thing was that while I didn't want him to kiss me, I realized I'd like to continue seeing him because he could be nice and fun to be with. None of it made sense.

Would Lee have been as ill at ease with my friends as I was with his? I didn't know for sure.

Maybe, I mused, the older you were, the more easily you could adapt to a situation. The night at Sonny's when Jill Rogers beckoned to Lee, he'd joined a high school crowd and he seemed to enjoy himself. His date then, Maureen, was a college student, though. Perhaps later, when they were alone, they snickered about being with high school kids, but if they hadn't accepted the two vacant seats at our table, they'd have had to stand or to leave Sonny's.

My parents and I went upstairs, Mama and me walking in front with Dad lingering to check and be sure I'd bolted the door since I was the last one coming in. If I hadn't had so much on my mind I'd probably have teased my father, asking if he didn't think I was enough of an adult to remember to lock up.

But I didn't. I kept quiet. All of a sudden I wasn't sure how much of an adult I actually was. Compared to the people at the party, I might just as well have been in grade school. My self-confidence had been badly shattered, and thinking about the embarrassment of the night, I cringed.

After so many new experiences in one evening and with images of Lee and Mike jumbled together in my thoughts, I expected to have a difficult time getting to sleep, and just the opposite happened. The previous night had been awful and

I'd stayed awake for long stretches at a time, tortured with a million questions about the fight with Mike, reliving the hurt over what he and I said to one another. But as I undressed shortly after midnight Friday, I looked out of the bay window in my bedroom at the outline of the mountains in the distance. There was something very substantial about them even though I could only see a dark streak against the horizon.

A wave of fatigue engulfed me and it was all I could do to stay awake long enough to wash my face and brush my teeth. The bed felt delicious. Snuggling under the blankets, I vaguely remembered to turn off the lamp on the bedside table, and I must have lost consciousness at once.

XIV

Sleet clattering noisily against my bedroom windows roused me earlier Saturday morning than I wanted to be awake. It was just seven o'clock, the gray sky barely showing a hint of daylight. My first coherent thought was that the gift shop wouldn't have many customers if the bad weather continued all day.

As I sat up in bed, other thoughts crowded that one out. The events of Friday night came rushing back. Lee . . . the party . . . the jokes about his robbing the cradle . . . his intense kisses when he brought me home. . . .

And Mike. I could no more stop thinking about Mike Maxwell than I could have willed the sun to shine.

Lying down again, I found myself wishing it was a school day with the high school furnace fixed and Mike waiting in his usual spot when I stepped off the bus. He'd take my hand, his fingers warm on mine, and his eyes would glow with happiness simply because we were together.

I jerked myself into a sitting position again, swinging my feet to the floor and fumbling for my bedroom slippers. By then it was twenty minutes past seven and Mike would already be at the service station because he went to work much earlier than I did. Had he made breakfast? Or bought something from a quick food place or a vending machine? Or maybe he hadn't felt like eating. Had he dated Jill Friday night while I was at the party with Lee?

The questions were torture. *Don't keep thinking about Mike*, I ordered myself as I'd done so many times the past few days, knowing full well the order wouldn't be obeyed.

I dressed for work, and when I went downstairs, my mother was wearing her red housecoat as she usually did on gray mornings. She gave me a cheery greeting and said my timing was perfect as breakfast was on the table.

I found myself wishing Mike could share our food. He loved bacon cooked very crisp, and buttered toast with jam, and he thought my mother made marvelous scrambled eggs. "Nobody else gets them this creamy, Mrs. Jamison," he'd told her once. As I unfolded my napkin and put it in my lap, I could imagine how Mike would look if he'd been there in our kitchen sitting opposite me, his hand curling around his orange juice glass and his eyes as blue as the Blue Ridge Mountains on a clear day.

Mike. . . .

Dad's voice, addressing me, brought me back to reality. I was a little surprised to discover my plate was empty. I must have eaten mechanically, more engrossed in thinking of Mike than in tasting my food.

"Christy, I'm going into town this morning and I'll take you to the gift shop so your mother won't have to go out in such mean weather," Dad said.

"I can drive myself if Mama isn't planning to use her car —"

Before I finished the sentence, he shook his head. "This rain is part ice and if it keeps up, the road will be slick as glass by the time you come home tonight. I don't want you driving alone after dark, especially on a frozen highway."

The subject seemed to be closed as Dad carried his coffee into the den to finish drinking it while he watched the news on television. The motor plant he managed was in operation five days a week and on those mornings he left the house at seven, but on Saturdays he often went to his office for a few hours, saying he could take care of a lot of paper work when everything was quiet.

Mama and I remained at the breakfast table. She refilled her cup and I shook my head when she asked if I'd like more coffee.

"If you need a ride home tonight, call me," she said. "Your daddy or I will pick you up."

She seemed to assume that Mike would *not* bring me, and I knew she must be wondering if Lee would do it. I wondered about that, too.

Mama's eyes were on me as if she was waiting for me to speak, and I nodded, very busy folding my napkin to avoid looking at her. An uncanny silence filled the kitchen. Outside, the rain continued with its rattling sound, but she and I might as well have been sitting in a vacuum.

"Christy," she hesitated a fraction of a second, "how old is Lee Carlyle?"

I caught my breath. "I'm not sure. I — I haven't asked him."

"He looks to me as if he's at least twenty-one or two. And he's still dating high school girls?" Her voice was as filled with surprise, just the way Duncan's had been at the party when he accused Lee of robbing the cradle.

Every muscle in my body stiffened. To be doing something — doing anything — I picked up the paper napkin once more, opening and refolding it, rolling one of its corners between my thumb and forefinger.

"I really don't see that Lee's age is important," I said thinly. "I'm not exactly a child, you know."

"I realize that you aren't a child, Christy, and age won't be important when you're a little older, but you're still in high school and he's —" She stopped as if she wasn't sure how to continue.

"Well, Lee must be all right because I don't believe you'd be interested in going out with a boy who wasn't nice," she went on. "I hope you wouldn't. It's just that I'd hate for you to find yourself in a situation which was . . . awkward."

I continued to play with the paper napkin. It was a crumpled wad in my hands.

"Christy, what about Mike?" she asked.

Rain made a steady rhythm against the window. I had to answer my mother and didn't know what to tell her. All the oxygen seemed to be draining out of my lungs.

"I don't know about Mike," I mumbled, speaking the truth although she may have believed I was putting her off. A hard thumping began in my chest. "I don't know, Mama," I whispered. "I honestly don't."

She knew the question was upsetting to me, and she laid her hand over mine on the table, concern showing in her face. "I shouldn't have brought that subject up this time of day," she sighed.

"What does the time of day have to do with it?" I said in a faraway voice.

"I didn't mean to pry, Christy, but Mike is such a nice boy and I can't bear to see you troubled. This wasn't the best time for me to inquire about him, though. Or about Lee. Not when you're ready to go to work. Get your coat and boots because Bryan's news program will end any minute."

I suppose my father had business matters on his mind during the ride into Greenview that morning as he seemed preoccupied, but his silence was a blessing for me. I was relieved not to have to answer any more questions.

There were problems on my mind, also, and the first one would call for an instant solution since I'd be face to face with Lee shortly. I didn't know what to say to him after his ardent good night kiss. It seemed too impersonal to give him a mere, "Good morning," but I couldn't think of a greeting which was warmer than casual and yet wasn't flirtatious.

Dad, who wasn't driving fast, swerved to miss an icy place on the pavement, and I marveled at his seeing it in time to avoid skidding. Rain continued to fall and the mountains were lost behind a bank of murky, gray clouds. From time to time thin wisps of ice caught on the windshield wipers, melting quickly as the defroster was warming the glass. I was thankful my father was behind the wheel instead of my taking the car into town.

My anxiety about how to greet Lee intensified. Mike was the only boy I'd ever dated seriously, so I didn't have much experience where guys were concerned.

Betsy was the girl I knew best, but somehow it seemed disloyal to Mike to discuss Lee with her since she and Gordon were Mike's long-time friends. Besides, she didn't know about the trouble between Mike and me — unless Mike had told her or he'd talked it over with Gordon who repeated the conversation to her. I shivered, thinking about that possibility. I realized I would never have known Betsy as well as I did in such a short period of time if it hadn't been for my relationship with Mike, and even if I wanted to tell her about the party and Lee, there was no chance to do it as I'd see Lee very soon.

Everything seemed to be closing in until I felt as smothered in grayness as the mountains when Dad dropped me at the gift shop, but my worries proved to be futile. Lee acted just the same toward me as he had previously. He was polite and reasonably talkative without saying anything the least bit personal.

He was bustling around in the stockroom when I arrived, and after commenting, "Great weather for cold-natured ducks, isn't it?" a remark also addressed to Mrs. Gibson who came in at the same moment I did, he hoisted a cardboard carton to the work table and carefully slit the brown mailing tape binding it.

"I believe the merchandise in that box is for my department, Lee," Mrs. Gibson said as she glanced at the name of the sender. "I hope to heaven it's crystal salad plates. They're a staple for the shop, but we've been out of them for a week and I've had so many requests for those plates I'm beginning to think half the people in Greenview are giving them for Chrsitmas gifts."

"Half giving them and the other half getting them." Lee grinned. "Yep, you're right. Crystal salad plates coming right up. Christy," he looked at me and gestured to more cartons in the corner, "there are books for you in the freight shipment which came in yesterday. I think the bigger box has paperbacks, and I know that one" he pointed again, "must be full of hardcover books because it's as heavy as lead."

"Will you open them this morning?" I asked.

"Are you in a hurry?"

"I sold the last atlas in stock yesterday, and we're low on children's picture books again."

"Sure," he came back. "Will do. I'll get to them as soon as the salad plates are taken care of."

152

If the beginning was any indication, I told myself, it promised to be a routine day. I let my breath out slowly, thankful for Lee's not mentioning our date, never dreaming as I hung my coat beside Mrs. Gibson's and headed for the book department, that routine certainly would not be the correct term to describe the day's ending.

XV

It was, as all of us working in the gift shop had anticipated, a dull day so far as sales were concerned. The icy rain continued and only a handful of customers came in the store. There were very few cars on the street.

Shortly before noon Lee went out to do errands for his father, and Mrs. Gibson and I ate our sandwiches together in the stockroom, propping open the door leading into the shop so we'd be able to see any people who came in the front entrance. None did.

"Next week we'll probably be too busy to breathe," Mrs. Gibson said as she took her final bite. "This morning I heard the weather report on my way to work and the radio announcer said we're supposed to have sunshine every day next week. In fact, he even thinks it may clear up tonight."

"Sunshine can't come too soon to suit me," I murmured, gazing at the bleak, overcast sky. "I can endure the cold, but I've had it with rain and grayness."

I was relieved that Lee hadn't invited me to lunch, but at the same time, I felt a tinge of disappointment. During the morning I'd stayed out of the stockroom as much as possible in order not to be too near him, and when he brought books to me, Mrs. Gibson was always in hearing distance. He didn't get around to uncrating the hardcover books until early afternoon, and a few minutes before three, Mr. Carlyle suggested that I mark prices on them. Lee had stacked the hardcovers on the stockroom table.

"We'll have them ready in case business picks up Monday," Mr. Carlyle went on. "If Mrs. Gibson needs you in the shop, she'll call. Be sure to check the titles against the invoice list and make sure we received everything we ordered."

I was glad to be busy, but the checking was so routine it became boring. Counting a stack of books methodically, I affixed price stickers and moved on to the next stack. My mind was roving. I don't know why I should have thought of a particular episode, but I remembered the night Mike came to my house and helped shell peas. It happened back in the early summer when my mother's garden had produced more green peas than she expected. Shelling them was a dull chore — just as counting books was a dull chore. At least, the shelling was uninteresting until Mike appeared, and then it was fun because he and I did it together.

Mike. . . .

155

Thinking about him gave me a hollow feeling inside. I wondered if he'd had a busy day at the service station, or if, like the gift shop, customers were scarce. Did he think about me? Often? Occasionally? Was he too busy planning a big Saturday night date with Jill to dwell on me?

As I considered that possibility, a book slipped out of my fingers, giving a flat *plop*! when it hit the floor. I jumped at the sound.

After a while Lee came into the stockroom and took off his soaked raincoat, sending a spray of water in every direction.

"So it's still raining outside?" I asked just to be saying something.

"What else is new?" Lee grinned. "I don't believe it's quite as gray as it was at noon. Maybe that's a sign we won't have to build an ark."

Both of us smiled and I tried to think of a silly remark, but couldn't come up with anything. After counting another stack of books, I set them aside, very conscious that Lee was watching me.

"Christy, what about seeing a movie tonight?" he said.

For a split second I was silent, and before I could reply, Mr. Carlyle called to Lee from the office.

"I'll be back in a sec when I find out what Dad wants," Lee said to me. "Don't go 'way."

I leaned against the corner of the stockroom table, trying to sort out the jumble of thoughts racing through my mind. Going to the movies with Lee Carlyle would be far more interesting than sitting home in front of the television set and trying to pretend to Mama and Dad that I was happy.

Still, it wasn't Lee I longed to date. I had to admit that to myself. I ached to be with Mike once more . . . but I wasn't sure if Mike wanted me. The one thing I did know was that if I continued to date Lee, Mike's and my relationship was finished. Mike wouldn't want me to date another guy any more than I wanted him to date Jill.

I had to make a choice, and I couldn't delay. Suddenly, it hurt to think. Blood was pounding against my temples.

Lee was a nice person and I enjoyed having him for a friend, but it was Mike I loved and Mike I wanted. Mike's kisses warmed me, not Lee's.

Standing there in the stockroom by myself, I tried to think about what had gone wrong between Mike and me. Maybe I'd been too possessive. Maybe he merely wanted a friendship with Jill, the sort of friendship I'd like to have with Lee. After all, Mike's natural friendliness was one of his biggest charms, one of the first traits which drew me to him that long-ago January afternoon at the service station when I didn't even know his name. I wanted him to keep that friendliness. I didn't want him to change. I wanted him to be the same Mike I'd come to love.

Lee returned to the stockroom and said, "Dad just wanted to check on the phone bill because I'd made a couple of long-distance calls. Christy, about the movie tonight —" He paused and waited.

I made myself look at him, hoping I could say what had to be said, that he would understand. My heartbeats quickened and there was a rushing sound in my ears.

"I can't, Lee," I blurted out. "I — I really shouldn't have gone to the party with you last night because — because —" I began again. "It's not that I don't like you, because I do. I like you lost. But. . ."

"But what?" he asked when I hesitated.

"I'm going steady with another boy. At least, I *was* going steady." My voice wavered when I used the past tense. "He and I are — are sort of on the outs right now, but I don't want that to be permanent and it will be if I start dating other people. I — I hope you understand."

I couldn't continue staring at him. Ducking my head, I stared at a crack in the stockroom floor.

Lee cleared his throat. "Mike Maxwell?" he asked. "Is Mike the one?"

I nodded.

For a long minute neither of us spoke. I found myself wishing a customer would come into the shop and want books so I'd have an excuse to leave Lee, but as soon as the thought crystalized, I realized that wouldn't be good. It would only lengthen a difficult situation if I went away before Lee and I finished talking.

Lee broke the silence. "Mike's an okay guy," he said.

"I hope you and I can be friends."

"Sure, we can, Christy. You're honest. I'll say that for you. I guess you're using your brain which is more than I can say for myself when I was in a similar situation."

"I don't understand. What do you mean?"

"Do you remember Amy Rivenbark from the party last night?"

I nodded again.

"Amy and I used to date when we were in high school. We went steady for more than a year, and I was the one who let that come to an end." He bit down on his lower lip. "Since then, I've wished a million times I hadn't been so dumb. She even wrote me a couple of times when I was working for my uncle and I didn't bother to answer the letters. I meant to do it, but just kept putting it off."

It was a relief to be talking about Lee and Amy instead of about Mike and me. "Why don't you phone her?" I suggested. "Last night she seemed awfully glad to see you."

"Nope. It's too late now. I dropped a big hint to her last night about wanting to date her again, but she didn't go for the idea, and after I'd begged a while, she admitted she's in love with somebody else. She's a junior at Virginia Tech in Blacksburg and she said she's serious about a fellow she met there. He's from New Orleans and after Christmas she's going to Louisiana to meet his family."

"Lee, I'm sorry. Honest."

"Me, too," he sighed. "I had my chance with Amy once and muffed it. Oh, man, did I ever muff it!"

He appeared upset enough to make me think he needed to be by himself. Besides, I'd finished pricing the hardcovers and all the invoices had been checked.

"I suppose I should get back into the shop," I murmured.

"Thanks for leveling with me about yourself, Christy. A lot of people wouldn't be decent enough to do that. I'd rather know where I stand with you."

I tried to smile at him, but it couldn't have looked like much of a smile when my lips seemed to have turned to wood. *Too late now* . . . That phrase of Lee's was terrifying. As I left the stockroom and returned to the book department, I hoped desperately it wasn't too late for Mike and me to pick up where we'd left off before we began to quarrel.

Maybe, I told myself, there would be a miracle and Mike would be waiting outside the shop when I left work. He would kiss me and everything would be lovely between us. He'd say he didn't care anything about Jill.

All those thoughts were wishful thinking. The familiar hollow sensation in the bottom of my stomach made me feel woozy as I straightened a rack of books, and I faced up to the truth: I couldn't count on a miracle to make things right between Mike and me.

I had to try to create the miracle for us . . . and pray it wasn't already too late.

XVI

Only two customers came into the book section after I left Lee in the stockroom, and I waited on them as mechanically as if I'd been a robot, taking their money, giving them change, and slipping their purchases into paper bags. At any other time I'd have chatted, suggesting new books they might like, or at least making a comment about the weather or the problems of Christmas shopping — or about something.

By quarter past five I'd come to a decision. I knew what I had to do, and going to Mr. Carlyle's office, I asked him if I could leave work early. For some unknown reason, I was embarrassed.

"I'll make up the time next week by cutting my lunch period short," I said.

"If you cut that half-hour lunch break, Christy, you'll have time for a drink of water but not for food," he answered with a wry smile. "Yes, go on whenever you're ready. Lee can handle any customers — if we have any. And don't worry about making up what you miss today. I may even close the store early since we aren't doing enough business to warrant hanging around until six."

I didn't want another conversation with Lee at the moment or questions about my reason for stopping work ahead of schedule, something I'd never done before, and luckily, he wasn't in sight as I got my coat. Mrs. Gibson didn't question me, either. She was rearranging a display of small silver picture frames and I said, "See you Monday," and kept moving, heading for the door and not giving her a chance to reply.

The rain had stopped at last, although the sidewalk and street glistened with water. Twilight had already changed into an eerie winter darkness and the air seemed colder than it was when I came to work in the morning, but maybe I was so nervous I felt the penetrating chill more than I would have normally. At first, I walked swiftly, but after covering a short distance it took all my strength to lift my feet off the pavement. *If Mike turns his back on me and tells me to get lost . . .*

It was three blocks from the gift shop to the Greenview Service Station and as I completed the first block, my heart was thudding against my ribs. *Let me reach Mike before he leaves work, let me reach Mike before he leaves work,* I repeated over and over to myself. I could have called him from the gift shop to tell him I was coming, but what I wanted to say was too intimate to be spoken over the phone, and there was no guarantee of privacy in the shop. Or in the service station.

I guess, too, I didn't want him to hang up on

me. Mike wasn't usually rude, but he might not want to talk to me at all. Earlier, when I decided to attempt to create a miracle for Mike and me, I'd had a little more self-confidence, but as I trudged along on the wet pavement I wasn't sure of anything except a gnawing fear.

Instead of going straight to the front of the service station, I turned left after two blocks and rounded the corner so I could approach by the back. Mike parked in the rear just as the other employees did, and while he always locked the ignition, I knew he seldom locked his automobile doors when he was on the job. If I'd gone to the front of the station where the gas pumps were located, he and I would have been in view and I couldn't stand to think of our having an audience for whatever we said to one another. That would be awkward under any circumstances, and horrible if he wanted our breakup to be permanent.

An unpaved alley was located behind the service station and my boots made a squishing noise as I walked in the soft mud. Mike's car was just where I knew it would be. Two floodlights on the roof at the back of the service station kept the area from being pitch black although the beams didn't quite reach into Mike's sedan, and I was thankful for that.

I don't cry often, but that afternoon tears misted in my eyes and I blinked hard to make them go away. It was cold in the automobile and I sat huddled up on the familiar seat while I waited, my hands twisting in my lap. The lump which formed in my throat as I left the gift shop was growing.

A man's voice rang out, followed by laughter, and while I didn't understand the actual words which were spoken, I recognized the voice as belonging to one of the mechanics. Some of the service station lights went out. A door was shut hard and the knob rattled as if a person was making sure it was locked. Mr. Maxwell was closing for the night and his employees were leaving.

Footsteps sounded behind the car and without moving my head to look over my shoulder, I knew they belonged to Mike. My pulses quickened although they were already racing.

"Oh! What —?" Mike gave a startled gasp as he opened the car door and saw me.

I couldn't speak for a second. I don't even think I breathed although my lungs needed air. Mike and I just stared at each other.

"Do you mind?" I managed finally, my voice quivering.

"Oh, gosh, no, Christy! I just never dreamed . . . I mean, I didn't expect . . ."

The sentence died. He slid under the steering wheel but didn't start the motor. I had to say what I was thinking, saying it at once or explode.

"Mike, about the other night," I blurted out. "I'm sorry!"

"Me, too," he said softly. "These past couple of days have been the worst time of my entire life. I wanted to phone you, but I was — Well, I was scared you'd hang up on me."

"I wouldn't have. Didn't your mother tell you I called you late Thursday night?"

"No, she didn't!" His eyebrows went up in amazement. "She must have forgotten! If only I'd known —"

I believed him. Mrs. Maxwell wasn't very careful about relaying messages. Sitting beside him in the dark car, I knew all the doubts and fears I'd had wondering about his feeling for me were stupid.

"Christy, I even drove by your house," he said. "On the road, not up in the yard."

"When?"

"Late Thursday night. It was between ten and eleven o'clock."

"If you'd only come in, Mike . . ."

"I wanted to do it, but I was scared to ring the doorbell. I don't think of myself as a coward, but I wasn't brave enough to hear you tell me to get out of your life for keeps, and I figured you might."

"I'd never tell you that," I whispered.

There wasn't any reason for us to feel strange with each other, but at that moment, we did. I was aware of a growing shyness within myself and I could sense the same shyness in him. I wanted his arms around me, wanted the reassurance of his kisses, but I couldn't reach out to embrace him and he must have had the same reaction.

"It seems like a million years since Thursday," he mumbled.

I took a deep breath. "Mike, I — I have to tell

you something. Last night I had a date with Lee Carlyle."

"I know."

"You *what?*" It was my turn to gasp.

"The service station had a call from the state police asking us to send the wrecker to tow a stalled truck off the highway late yesterday afternoon, and Uncle Eb sent me to do it. I didn't get back until a little after six and as soon as I unloaded that truck I went to the gift shop to pick you up. It was later than usual, and when I came around the corner, I saw you getting into Lee's car with him."

"I wish you'd stopped."

"I figured Lee wasn't forcing you into his car, Christy. You must have been with him because you wanted to be there."

"I'd rather have been with you."

"You mean that? Honest?"

"Honest," I said. "Lee drove me home and then invited me to a party some friends of his were having and I went, but it wasn't much fun."

"Why not?"

"All the others were college students and they teased me about still being in high school, then teased Lee about robbing the cradle. But I guess the real reason it wasn't much fun was that I was thinking about you the entire time."

"Then you're not wrapped up in Lee?"

"I like him — as a friend. He asked me for a date for tonight but I refused."

The silence was back between us, and so was

the awkwardness. "What about you, Mike?" I asked. I didn't say, *Were you with Jill?* but I was thinking the question.

"I didn't do anything. Both nights I came back to the service station. Uncle Eb was working and I helped him put new plugs in a couple of pickup trucks, but it's a miracle I didn't do everything backward because I couldn't think of anything except how much I wanted to be with you."

"Oh, Mike...."

"Listen, Christy, there's something we need to get straight once and for all." His grip on my hands tightened and his voice was firm. "I got mad with you Thursday because you were assuming Jill and I had a big romantic deal going, and that's not how it is. Sure, I dated her a while back, but that was before I knew you. When I met you and went out with you a few times, I realized Jill was just a friend and that you were the one I wanted to be with."

I must have leaned toward him and I guess he swayed toward me because I felt the familiar warmth of his arms. We held each other close, not kissing, just clinging together, his heartbeats so loud in my ears they almost blotted out mine.

Both of us realized at the same minute that we were in a very public place. I pulled back, and he dropped his arms but he found my hands again, holding them in his big, warm palms.

"It's probably more private at your house," he said softly.

I felt as if I'd been on a long, treacherous journey and was home at last because Mike and I were together.

"I'll even invite you to stay for supper," I told him.

"You don't have to beg me. Will it be okay with your folks? I wouldn't want to make your mother mad by coming without advance notice."

I actually giggled, remembering how Mama looked at breakfast when she asked about Mike and said, "Mike is such a nice boy." I knew instinctively she and Dad would be delighted that things were right between Mike and me again.

"She won't be mad," I told him. "If you'd like to know the truth, I rather think she's going to be ecstatic." Resting my cheek on his shoulder for a second, I added, "I'll be ecstatic, too."

Mike started the motor, steering the car with one hand because his other arm was around me. I felt warm and peaceful, knowing I'd made the right choice.

This is growing up, I found myself thinking as we rode through Greenview. Facing problems instead of hiding from them or making excuses . . . seeking solutions . . . trying to see situations from another person's point of view. Mike's *liking* Jill as a friend didn't stop him from *loving* me any more than my friendship with Lee Carlyle meant I no longer cared for Mike.

Mike made an expert one-handed turn from the road into the lane leading up our hill, and I thought about his description of my house. "The house with all the crazy windows," he'd called it that long-ago January afternoon at the service station when he asked where I lived and I'd told him although I didn't even know his name. Now, golden light streamed from those bay windows, a welcome for us as he braked near the back steps in a shadowy spot.

"Look, Christy, there's a star," he said, glancing up at the sky. "It's rained so much lately I don't know when I saw a star last."

"Let's make a wish on it."

"I don't need to wish now," he answered tenderly. "My wishes have just come true."

So have mine, I thought as he kissed me.